Harpier's Pawn

Harpier's Pawn

Red House

A Novel

The first book in the Harpier's Pawn Trilogy

Daniel Christian Green

iUniverse, Inc.
New York Lincoln Shanghai

Harpier's Pawn
Red House

Copyright © 2007 by Daniel Christian Green

All rights reserved. No part of this book may be used or reproduced by any means, graphic, electronic, or mechanical, including photocopying, recording, taping or by any information storage retrieval system without the written permission of the publisher except in the case of brief quotations embodied in critical articles and reviews.

iUniverse books may be ordered through booksellers or by contacting:

iUniverse
2021 Pine Lake Road, Suite 100
Lincoln, NE 68512
www.iuniverse.com
1-800-Authors (1-800-288-4677)

Because of the dynamic nature of the Internet, any Web addresses or links contained in this book may have changed since publication and may no longer be valid.

This is a work of fiction. All of the characters, names, incidents, organizations, and dialogue in this novel are either the products of the author's imagination or are used fictitiously.

ISBN: 978-0-595-46067-0 (pbk)
ISBN: 978-0-595-90365-8 (ebk)

Printed in the United States of America

For my late wife Julia and her children—Sookei, Jonathan, Kendi, and Denice. Death and borders may keep us apart but my heart is with you every day.

And for anyone who has lost a loved one at the hands of the wicked, their time will come.

"You can kill dozens of men in war and be called a hero, but kill one man for destroying your life and they'll call you a murderer."

—Pvt. Carl Austin Byrd
1915–1991

Chapter 1

Tin Soldiers

November 3rd, 2007

Eight policeman dressed in paramilitary gear listened intently as their longtime friend and secret business partner, Federal Agent Larry Jones, mapped out the details of the unauthorized raid they were about to carry out. Although respected members of law enforcement, these men led double lives infested with greed and murder.

Rarely would they risk stepping out of the shadows to take care of "problems" that might expose them and their illegal business ventures, but in this case there was no alternative. Time was running out.

Larry spoke quietly as he pointed across the open field to an old farmhouse in the distance. "The guy in that house is a cold-blooded killer. We won't have any problem justifying this raid … and I want him dead! If he's found old man Ybalde's notes we're done for. He should be alone and, judging from his MO, he's not heavily armed. This should be a piece of cake, so let's get this over with before my partner arrives."

The men checked their weapons and began to creep through the tall, grassy field towards the house. Larry stopped one of the men with a pat on the shoulder. "Jared, you stay here in case Miguel shows up before we're through."

Jared looked puzzled, "What if he does?"

Larry's face had a grave expression as he replied, "Make it quick."

Jared nodded, "No problem, Larry … he won't feel a thing."

Larry turned and made his way behind the advancing officers as they moved silently through the early morning mist towards the farmhouse.

As the team moved on the house, a series of large blasts echoed from the second story of the structure. The team watched with surprise as the lifeless form of a man flew out of an upstairs window in a shower of broken glass.

The moment of motionless silence was broken as one of the men's voices came through Larry's earpiece. "I thought you said he was alone! Do you think he knows we're here?"

Larry's eyes carefully analyzed the window as he watched for movement. Then he slowly pressed the microphone, "I don't know ... but we're definitely sitting ducks out here. *Let's move!*"

The team rose from their crouched positions and broke into a dead run towards the farmhouse, their sub-machine guns cutting dotted trails into and around the second story windows as they descended on the house, surrounding the structure.

Larry's voice was now frantic as he approached the front door. "Flash him and gas him!"

The team answered the given order instantly, hurling suppression grenades through the windows at the unseen foe. The quiet interior of the musty old farmhouse suddenly came alive in a swirling, blinding cloud of teargas and smoke.

As the choking occupant stumbled across the living room floor, he frantically jerked open a hatch leading to a tunnel under the chaotic firestorm that roared around him. He knelt down to lower himself into the tunnel when a flash grenade exploded behind him, sending him sprawling to the cold damp ground below with a thud.

"Dammit!" he screamed as he grabbed the door's rope and pulled hard, slamming the trap door shut, separating him from the turmoil above. He rested for a moment with his back against the tunnel wall and shook his head trying to counter the effects of the flash grenade.

He steadied his breath and moved his burning eyes to the wound he had received from the man that he had blown out of the window. Pressing his hand hard against it to slow the bleeding, he struggled to his all fours and began to crawl to the tiny point of light at the end of the tunnel.

His thoughts turned from confusion to anger over the events that had just occurred as he pulled a cell phone from the pocket of his gray trench coat and dialed a number.

Agent Miguel Perez opened his phone and greeted the caller in his usual professional tone, only to be cut short by an angry voice on the other end.

"I thought you were coming alone, Miguel! I suppose this is what you meant by talking!"

Miguel was stunned at the man's ranting words. "Who is this? What are you talking about?"

The killer shook his head and clenched his teeth at Miguel's questions. "Oh, I suppose you don't know anything about the men who, as we speak, are raiding the house you were supposed to meet me in?" Wait, let me guess … I'll bet you have absolutely no clue about the man who put a bullet in my side either? Well, guess what's happening now! Their blood is on your hands! Goodbye!"

Miguel's mind began to race as he tried to figure out what was going on. Suddenly his eyes grew wide in terror at the stark realization of what was about to happen.

"Jones! Oh, my god!" he said aloud as he slammed on the accelerator and raced down the country road.

Six years … six long years of a twisted puzzle of death left by a killer known only as the "Texas Motel Killer" was on it's way to being solved. It had been only a few days earlier when the almost ghost of a man had called and asked to meet him. But now the assurance Miguel had felt about ending his bloody rampage was replaced with a cold, sick feeling as he drew nearer to the old farmhouse.

Officer Jay Burk took aim through his scope at the car that was speeding down the dusty driveway. He knew Larry had told him to make it quick, but he had had several altercations with the young FBI agent over the past year. Larry had always backed him off of Miguel before, but this time Larry was not around.

The rifle reported, sending the well-aimed round accurately into the front tire of Miguel's car. The soft sand underneath the blown tire abruptly jerked the car sideways, sending it off the road and smashing into a line of trees with a shriek of torn metal.

"Bull's-eye!" Burk muttered to himself as he stood from his hidden position and leisurely strolled towards the car with his Beretta 9mm pistol in his hand.

Tiny beams of light pierced the cracks and holes in the old, smoke-filled house as the eight men silently slipped inside. Larry's eyes moved with his weapon as he scanned the room. With a quick hand gesture from him, the team carefully made their way through the bottom level of the house, searching every corner.

"He's not here, Sir. Just stacks of ammo cans in every room."

Larry's eyes moved to the staircase. A smile crept across his face as he pressed the microphone. "There's only one place he could be. Like I said, fellas, piece of cake."

The team crept up the stairs and down the narrow hallway to the only room at the end. Then, with a crash the door flew open and the team stormed into the room with their sub-machine guns blazing into every corner.

Larry's face froze with fear as he spotted a pulsating green light atop a large ammo can. Then a paralyzing thought slammed into his mind. This was a bomb … and the house was probably loaded with them.

"*Get out! Get out! It's a trap!*" he screamed as the men raced down the hall.

Larry had reached the staircase when a violent force took him off his feet and slammed him against the wall across the room. He hit the floor with a thud and tried to get to his feet but a sharp pain made him cringe as he saw the bone sticking out of his broken leg. His eyes moved around the living room floor where the motionless bodies of his seven team members lay strewn about like rag dolls.

He quickly turned onto his stomach and began to crawl when he noticed that the half-destroyed room was alive with tiny green dots from armed explosive devices. He let out a helpless whimper as he frantically dragged himself to the front door. With a grunt he reached for the doorknob, but it was too late as the boxes unleashed their furious swarms of flaming shrapnel, splintering the house into pieces and flinging what was left of the now dead Federal Agent end over end into the grassy field.

Officer Burk's pistol pressed hard against Miguel's temple as he spoke to the dazed agent. "Having a bad day, Miguel? Well, it just got worse."

Miguel's eyes widened as he heard the hammer click back on the Beretta.

The smiling officer's head quickly whipped around at hearing the deafening explosion coming from the field behind him. His mouth dropped in disbelief as his eyes reflected the sight of the old farmhouse disappearing into a rising cloud of flame and debris.

Seizing the opportunity, Miguel grabbed the pistol and forced himself out of the car onto the bewildered officer. The two men viciously wrestled for the weapon as they rolled on the ground. Still groggy from the wreck, Miguel was easily overpowered by Burk. His lightning fast hands snatched the pistol and struck Miguel in the jaw, flattening him on the ground. Burk rose to his feet and recocked the pistol as Miguel raised his hands.

"Why are you doing this, Burk? Where's Larry?"

Officer Burk sneered as he raised the weapon and aimed it at Miguel. "Larry's dead! You did this! Now, it's your turn!"

Miguel's eyes shifted from Burk's face to something behind him.

Burk felt a chill as a shadow towered over his own on the ground. He shouted and spun his weapon around when a choking pain hit him in the throat. He tried to scream but only a gargling gasp came out as his eyes met the veiled face of the killer who had struck him in the neck with the wide, razor-edged blade of his Ka-Bar Warthog knife.

Burk's eyes began to glass over as his life slipped away at the hands of the silent man that stood staring at his dying face. The officer's arms fell to his side and the Beretta slipped from his grasp. With a quick withdrawal, the killer pulled the knife free in a spray of blood, sending Burk's small, skinny form dropping to the sandy road.

Without a word, he wiped the knife clean on Burk's jacket and sheathed it. Then with his left hand he calmly picked up the Beretta pistol and uncocked it.

Fear crept over Miguel as he had the killer in full view for the first time. A large man with piercing eyes stared coldly from under the lip of his fedora hat. An old, white veil like that of a surgeon's mask covered the lower half of his face, making his eyes seem that much more menacing.

Holding the dead man's pistol, he stepped over Burk's body with his flat-nosed black boots and walked towards Miguel. As he approached, a gentle breeze blew open the tall man's trench coat exposing an array of weapons.

"If you're going to kill me, *just do it*! I'm not afraid of Death!" Miguel thundered as the man stood over him.

The killer chuckled as he slid the pistol into his coat pocket. "Kill you? If I wanted you dead, I would have let your friend over there do it. No, I don't want to kill you, Miguel, but you are going to have to take a little nap."

With his left hand he pulled a syringe out of his pocket and knelt down in front of Miguel's bleeding face. "We had a meeting, remember? You still want to talk, don't you?"

Miguel, still lightheaded from the car wreck and ensuing fight with Burk, weakly nodded his head in acknowledgement.

"Good!" the killer said as he injected the sedative into Miguel's neck with a quick movement. Miguel's vision blurred as the drug coursed through his veins, leaving him limp and unconscious on the dusty road.

Chapter 2

Fragile Dreams

February 3rd, 2000

A young man walked across the Mexican border. A smile spread across his face as he paced across the high concrete bridge that crossed the Rio Grande. He stopped halfway and pulled out a photo.

As he studied the picture of himself and his ex-wife, his mind wandered back to the failed marriage some two years earlier that had sent him in a tailspin of self-destruction ever since.

She was a strikingly beautiful woman who at first seemed to truly love him. Whether she really ever did would always remain a mystery to him as the angel that had promised him forever soon turned into a bitter, cold-hearted creature, leading him to a life of misery.

Not wanting to give up on his doomed relationship, the young man had started work as a truck driver to provide her with more money and give her some space. Unfortunately for him, the old cliché trucker stories he heard from fellow drivers about coming home to find their wives in compromising situations came true for him when he came in too early one night.

The usual chain of events followed, including a nasty divorce that cost him everything but the clothes on his back and his job. After all was said and done, the young man sank into a world of solitude. Every day, the never-ending stretch of highway was his escape from the torrential dismay that filled his mind. Even after the divorce, his ex-wife reassured him he was not to blame, but he could not shake the feeling that he could have done more to save his marriage. Nevertheless, it was over and he continuously searched for ways to dull his guilt-riddened mind.

He looked at the picture in his hand one last time. Then from his wallet he pulled out the ring that his first wife had given him back after the divorce. "Time to let it go," he muttered as he tossed the ring and photo into the river below.

He raised his hand and gazed at another gold ring that now bound him to his new family. Then he looked at his watch. Tonight was the night they were coming home with him … coming home to the United States, far away from the poverty and fear in Mexico.

"Two more hours," he thought to himself as he turned and walked across the bridge. A wide smile reflected his new-found happiness as he stepped into the US Customs Station.

January 1st, 1998

Two truckers walk into the Santa Maria truck stop in Laredo, Texas. The younger man was listening intently to the road stories of the old gray-bearded driver who was eager to converse with the quiet young man.

"Hey, are you hungry? I'm starving!" he said to the young, longhaired man as they entered the truck stop.

"Actually, I am … is the food any good here?"

The old man laughed loudly and slapped his new friend on the back. "It's alright … if it don't kill ya," he said as they sat down at a table and continued to talk.

The old man stared at the young man's face across the table and rubbed his bearded chin, thinking of what direction he could take the conversation. "What club do you like best in ol' Boy's Town?"

The young man tilted his head at the question. "Boy's Town? Where's that at?"

The old man chuckled at the young man's response. "You mean to tell me you've never been to Boy's Town? Oh man, I can't believe this! You are green."

The young man raised his hand curiously. "What's so special about Boy's Town? Where is it?"

The old man laughed again and reached across the table, patting the young man on the shoulder. "It's about four miles south of the border. Anything you want, you can get. I'll tell you what, let's eat supper and I'll take you down there … my treat. I still can't believe you don't know about Boy's Town."

The two men stepped out of a cab in the small Mexican town. The young man's eyes widened with amazement as he took in the street of endless clubs … and the many beautiful senoritas that flooded the dirt road leading into this almost heavenly place.

"Ya see, I told ya! Any fantasy with a woman you can think of is right here. All you need is money and imagination! Hey, let's go in here … this is the classiest cathouse in Mexico. Pappagallo's is a little more expensive, but you get what you pay for … if you know what I mean!"

The old man grinned and led the young man inside the noisy, smoky club.

The young man slowly scanned the room. His eyes moved from one smiling woman to another. He wanted them all as voice from behind the bar snapped him out of his trance. He turned his head towards the bulky, stone-faced man who leaned forward and spoke again, "Hey, sonny? You deaf?"

The young man blinked and answered, "No, Sir. I've just never been here before."

The bartender's stone face broke into a wide smile. "First timer, huh? Tell you what … the first drink is on me. What'll you have?"

The young man spoke instantly, "Vodka. Straight."

The bartender cocked his head and grabbed a bottle of Oso Negro and poured a shot. "There you go … enjoy! By the way, my name is Ruben … I run this place. Anything I can do for you, feel free to ask. One more thing … try not to listen to that old bastard behind you … he's crazy!"

The young man turned to his friend who was laughing at Ruben's comment. He grinned at the old man as he quickly downed the vodka shot and turned his attention to a dark-haired woman who was staring at him. "Boy's Town!" he whispered to himself as he grabbed another drink and walked towards the smiling woman.

July 5th, 1999

The morning sun slowly crept through the window of the rundown motel room that sat across the dusty road from Pappagallo's. The bright, silent beam glided across three sleeping bodies in a wrecked bed, coming to rest on the face of a young man. He blinked and winced as the daylight stung his swollen eyes.

With a shaking hand he reached out to close the curtain in an attempt to avert the light that added more misery to his already pounding head. Sighing, he flopped back on the bed, tossed for a moment and tried to return to his slumber but the growing headache made it impossible. He angrily tossed off the covers and sat on the edge of the bed holding his head in his hands. "Damned vodka!" he muttered to himself as he got up and staggered to the bathroom.

As he reached the bathroom door, he tripped on a beer bottle and almost fell. He held on to the old wooden doorframe, regaining his balance. Now fully awake, he peered around the hazy room. Condom wrappers, beer bottles and clothes lay strewn about. He turned his head and stared at the two prostitutes that lay sleeping on the bed, unstirred by the noise of his stumbling.

It seemed like he had been here all of his life. At first this was a haven of peace ... an oasis where he could stop the endless race he was running with his disappointing past. Unfortunately, the result was the same as everything else he had tried. This town had done nothing more than lead him right back to the same miserable life he had been living ... a life filled with heartache, guilt and self-loathing.

The liquor had become tasteless and the cocaine he shoveled up his nose by the spoonfuls ceased to numb out the wreckage of his past. The women, their beauty and charm, once drowned out every thought of his failed relationship and the feeling of loneliness. Now it had all become mundane, and sex became a mechanical act. Void of any feeling or emotion, the empty hole in his heart ached for real love ... something he had never really experienced.

He hung his head and sighed, closing the bathroom door with a click. The massive amount of alcohol he had consumed swelled in his stomach and now made it's way up his throat and into his mouth. He grunted and fell to his knees, vomiting loudly as he held the toilet seat tightly. His head pounded wildly. He fell backwards against the bathtub with a thud, whimpering softly from the pain in his stomach.

He sat there for a moment tilting his head back, hoping the bitter pain would subside. Then with trembling arms, he pulled himself off of the floor and to the sink. He turned on the hot water and splashed his face to soothe the headache, then slowly lifted his head looking at his reflection in the mirror.

"What have I become?" he thought to himself as he stared into eyes that were sunk deep into sockets that were almost black. His pale skin, once tanned, looked almost dead as a result of the copious quantities of chemicals he had ingested and long, sleepless nights.

A rush of anger came over him as he thought of the dreams in life he had as a boy. His life should have been very different ... but now it was barely worth living. He spit at the face in the mirror and punched his reflection, breaking the glass into sharp shards tinkling on the floor. He looked down at the blood oozing from his knuckles. His hand should be hurting. The fact that it wasn't made him chuckle as he sat down on the edge of the bathtub. "I don't want to be here anymore," he said aloud as he leaned forward and stared at the old green tile floor.

Then it hit him. He would end it … end it today. Death scared him, but it couldn't be any worse than what he was feeling right now.

Taking a deep breath, he stood and walked back into the room. He picked up his clothes and dressed himself. As he turned the doorknob he looked once more at the two sleeping women on the bed. They would not care. Hell … at this point no one cared. Present company included.

The young man opened the door and walked out into the already hot Mexican morning air. His boots plodded across the dusty road as he approached the bar.

Something caught his attention as he reached the first step to the club. He strained his eyes at the strange sight. A white owl sat on a post no more than ten feet from him. A chill ran through him that forced his swollen eyes shut. He opened them to see that the bird was no longer there. He looked around the empty town and shook his head. "Crazy!" he thought to himself as he walked into the bar.

Ruben Servin was busy chipping ice, preparing for the day when behind him he heard the bar door open. "We don't open 'til noon. Come back later," he said in a mild voice.

"I know you're not open, Jackass. Give me a drink!"

Ruben whipped around on the longhaired man with an irritated look. He shook his head and scolded him, "Didn't you have enough last night? I mean you could barely walk out of here! Go back to sleep and come in when I open like everyone else."

The young man seemed to be ignoring him, so Ruben threw down his cleaning rag and walked behind the counter, cursing under his breathe as he approached the man. "I said I'm not open yet. If you keep coming in like this everyone will come in early and I don't like opening early. So come back later!"

The longhaired man raised his bobbing head and looked into Ruben's face. "I don't care … I want a drink. I want a bottle of Oso Negro … and after that I want another one … and I want you to keep them coming … and until I get it, I will sit right here!"

Ruben grumbled as he turned and grabbed the bottle of vodka from the shelf and slammed it down in front of the man. "You know, Oso, if you keep drinking this crap like you do, you won't be alive much longer. Look at you! You're a mess! Why don't you go back to the states and chill out for a while? Find a nice girlfriend or something … you're only how old? 26?"

The young man nodded his head and looked at the bottle, slowly unscrewing the cap. "I have all the women I need right here."

Ruben's nostrils flared at the statement. "You mean these bitches? They only love one thing, and that's money. Hell, they're all taking bets on when you will die. Think about it, Cavron! You drink so much of this shit, it's your nickname. If I didn't have such a good memory, I wouldn't even know your real name."

The longhaired man leaned back in his seat and sighed. "Okay, mom … I'll be a good boy tomorrow, but right now can you please give me a shot glass? Please?"

Ruben shook his head and got a shot glass from under the counter, holding it in front of the young man. "You know, Oso, I pray for you every night. I pray that you would find what makes you happy … and I think God will answer my prayer. He can work miracles. Even for you."

The young man chortled and snatched the glass from Ruben. "Prayer? Miracle? Whatever, dude. I'll tell you what … if a miracle happens for me, Ruben, you'll be the only one to see it."

Ruben walked back to the ice chest and began to finish his work. The young man realized that Ruben was trying to ignore him, as he usually did when he started to make remarks about religion, so he continued with the task at hand and poured the first shot slowly. He had gently raised it to his lips when the bar door opened.

The bright morning sun still hurt his eyes, making him turn his head as he tried to see who was standing in the doorway. His first thoughts were to curse the person, but instead his eyes widened at the sight of a young Mexican woman.

The woman had a little girl by her side as she stepped into the bar and began to speak in Spanish to Ruben. The young man did not understand what was said, but listened anyway as Ruben answered her and shook his head. The woman nodded, and turned with a pitiful look on her face.

As she turned to leave, her eyes met the young man's. Something in her eyes made him temporarily lose his breath as they locked stares for a brief moment. Then she grabbed the little girl by the hand and walked back out into the hot July sun.

Feeling a rush of rejuvenation, the young man whipped his head around to Ruben and spoke with excitement, "Who was that?"

Ruben sighed, and raised his hand to his forehead. "She's from town. Trust me, she's not your type. She's not a whore."

The young man slapped his hand on the bar. "Dammit, Ruben! Who is she?"

Ruben looked curiously at his friend. He had never seen him this enthusiastic about anything. "Her name is Mayella. Her husband got killed a couple of years ago." Ruben returned to his work as he talked. "I'm telling you, Oso. She's a good girl. You don't like those kind, remember?"

Ruben heard the bar door slam and looked over at the empty seat where the young man had been sitting. The only thing there was the shot glass, still full of the strong vodka. He looked at the door, then back to the seat and broke into a wide smile. He then pointed his finger at the sky and spoke, "Ahhh, Dio! Gracious … gracious." Making the sign of the cross on his chest, he returned to his daily chores.

The bar door swung open and the young man stepped outside, searching the street for the woman. He turned his head towards Nuevo Laredo, and there she was. Wasting no time, he bolted down the dirt road in her direction, shouting for her to stop.

The young woman turned towards the running man and pushed her daughter behind her as he came to a halt.

He heaved from the hot day air as he caught his breath. His eyes studied her face as he tried to think of something to say. She was plain, not like the women that worked in the club, and she had a long scar on the left side of her face, but for some reason, she was the most beautiful thing he had ever seen.

"What you want?" the girl asked him in a defensive voice as he stood silently staring at her face.

He snapped out of his momentary trance and stammered, "I … I seen you back there in the club."

The woman narrowed her eyes and fired back, "I not a whore! Leave me alone!"

The young man raised his hands defensively and shook his head. "No! No, no … I don't want that. I just want to talk."

The woman sneered and turned around.

Knowing that he was looking foolish, he quickly tried to redeem himself. "Hey listen, are you hungry?"

The little girl pulled at her mother's dress and spoke. "I hungry."

The woman's eyes began to tear up as she looked at her daughter's smiling face. She was hungry too, but she would not lower herself like the other women in this desperate town.

The young man now saw an opportunity. He usually would not sink so low as to use a child to win a woman's favor, but he had to know her. The new-found life that now ran through his veins would not allow him to walk away.

"Okay, I will talk to you, but you no trick me. Understand?"

He gratefully agreed and the three began to walk towards the city.

"I forgot to introduce myself," he said calmly.

"I know who you are. You are the one that drinks too much," she said as she rubbed her daughter's hair.

He hung his head at her words and blushed with shame.

The woman looked up at the pitiful look on his face and giggled, "It's okay, lot of people drink too much. My mother used to say it's because they no like themselves."

The young man felt relieved by her words of understanding. "You know a lot of English, where did you learn it?" he asked.

"My father was American. He taught me some English, but I forget a lot of it. He was a bad man. He left us a long time ago."

"I never got your name," the young man asked.

She turned and looked up into his face. He seemed so eager to hear what she had to say. There was something about him, the way he looked at her. His eyes reminded her of her long-dead husband. She had loved no other man since his death, but something was strangely attractive about the tall man that walked beside her now. "My name is Mayella and this is my daughter Isabella," she said as they neared the city of Nuevo Laredo.

The young man looked down at the little girl who was smiling at him from behind her mother's worn dress. He had a thought. With a quick grab he reached down and picked up Isabella and plopped her up on his shoulders. The little girl squealed with excitement and laughed out loud at the gesture. Mayella gave the man a puzzled look.

He looked at her and shrugged his shoulders. "At least one of us won't be tired!"

Mayella's quizzical look turned to a smile as they walked into the restaurant.

February 3rd, 2007–10 pm

The young man sat anxiously in his idling Kenworth cabover at the designated spot Ruben had told him he would bring Mayella and Isabel to. A sickening feeling that something was wrong crept over him as he stepped out of his truck and walked towards the fence.

"Where the hell are you, Ruben!" he thought to himself as he stared out into the cold darkness, wondering why Rueben was late.

He turned to walk back to his truck when a flash in the corner of his eye caught his attention. A large white owl sat on an old wooden post where the original border fence used to stand. Slowly, he stepped towards the large bird. Unblinking, the bird fixed its stare directly into his eyes.

Being raised in the country, he could not believe he was this close to a wild owl as he reached out and touched the owl's soft white feathers with his trembling fingers.

Suddenly, the silent moment of amazement was cut short by a car horn honking wildly from the Mexican side of the border fence.

Without warning the bird of prey became airborne and flew by the startled young man, scratching his face with it's talons as it flew by. A strange warmth flooded through his body as he touched the burning wound left by the owl. The night began to spin and his ears were filled with a deafening sound of what seemed like thousands of whispering people. He shook his head and fell to his knees as the whispers turned into a flurry of blood-curdling screams. He pressed hard against his ears hoping to block them out, but it was no use. Then just as suddenly as it started, the voices stopped. Only the sound of the approaching car could be heard in the windy night.

A hard lump formed in his throat as he recognized the shape of Ruben's car. His legs seemed to move by themselves as he ran through the hole he had cut in the fence and to the stopped vehicle.

Ruben stumbled out of the car and fell to his knees crying as the young man reached him.

"Where are they, Ruben? Where is Mayella? Where is Isabel? *Where are they?*" his anger exploded as he pulled the big Mexican man from the ground and to his feet.

His eyes donned an eerie glow that frightened Ruben, whose voice was shaky as he began to speak. "I tried to stop them, Oso. I tried, but they took them."

The young man noticed that Ruben's hands were covered in blood. His confusion turned to shock as the realization that something awful had happened to his wife and daughter spun in his brain.

Ruben hugged his friend and, with a sobbing voice, sadly told him the events of the past few hours.

The young man grabbed his long hair in his hands and pressed hard against his head as he began to wail like a wounded animal. He started to walk, but stumbled to his knees.

Ruben could only look on in sadness as his friend began to break apart as if his very soul was being ripped from him.

Ruben looked down at the wound he had received earlier. The blood was black, meaning he had been shot through the liver. He did not have much time. He turned his head back towards the city he had just come from to see a series of flickering lights approaching in the distance. Ruben looked back at the young man who was now swaying back and forth in an almost catatonic state.

If he left him here the men in the approaching cars would surely kill the young man, but if he took his friend to safety in the US, the time it would take would prove fatal for him from the wound he had received.

The hulking man made his decision quickly and picked up his youthful friend, carrying him on his big shoulders to the idling big rig. Ruben held his hand tightly against his abdomen as he put the truck in gear. He looked out the window and saw that the car lights were less than a mile away. "You bastards! You'll get yours!" he thought to himself as he drove off into the night.

Chapter 3

The Meeting

Miguel slowly opened his eyes. A sharp pain ripped through his side from the broken ribs he had received from the car wreck. He moved to hold them for support, but his hands were strapped down to the arms of a wooden chair that sat underneath him. Instinctively, he tried to stand, but to no avail as his legs were also bound to the chair.

He raised his swimming head and looked around the room where he sat. Only a small lamp dimly lit up the cinder block walls that surrounded him. Above his head were a series of pipes that slowly dripped water in small puddles on the concrete floor. He guessed it to be an old basement of some kind, judging by the thick rust on the pipes and small mounds of mildewed mortar that fell from between the blocks.

Miguel speculated for a moment that maybe this was some crazy nightmare, but unfortunately it was all too real.

He had a thought that made him chuckle painfully. Miguel had always hated his office in Dallas. It was cramped but right now it seemed like heaven compared to this freezing room he was imprisoned in.

Another thought struck him. His partner, Larry, was now dead.

"My God … Larry," he muttered as he hung his head, imagining his fellow agent's death, and wondered why Larry had taken it upon himself to show up at the farmhouse ahead of him.

The sound of boots clicking down the concrete hall outside the room made him lift his head towards a steel door a few feet away. A feeling of nausea swept over him as he realized the utterly helpless position he was in. He gripped the chair's arms tightly as he steadied himself for whoever was about to walk in. The heavy metal door opened with a creak as a large, dark figure entered the room.

Miguel blinked and slowly focused his eyes on the ominous form. The man had the appearance of a gangster from the 1930s ... a Fedora hat sat atop his bald-shaven head, only revealing the man's piercing brown eyes, and a gray trench coat hung from his shoulders that was open, exposing an array of weapons. A blood-stained bandage was wrapped around his abdomen.

Miguel glimpsed the man's eyes as he held out a water bottle in his gloved hand and shook it. They seemed to be burning a hole through him with their motionless gaze.

"Thirsty?" inquired the man.

Miguel decided to stick to his police training. He would have to play it tough to discover the man's intentions towards him. "No, I am not thirsty. Listen, Sir, you have no idea how much trouble you've brought down on yourself. You need to let me go and turn yourself in before this gets any worse. Right now the entire Bureau is looking for me and I don't have to tell you what will happen to you if you don't cooperate."

The cloaked man cocked his head and began to laugh, setting the water down in order to hold the bullet wound in his side.

Miguel blushed with anger as the man fought off his laughter and spoke, rubbing his eyes. "Please ... excuse me, Miguel. It's just that I've read many of your operations training manuals and I didn't realize how ridiculous some of your crisis responses were until just now. As for finding me, your Bureau has been looking for me for seven years now. I really doubt they'll find me in the next few hours."

The man chuckled under his breath and grabbed a chair. "Let's move on to the next topic, shall we?"

Miguel was now filled with rage as he answered, "What topic?"

The man sat gingerly in the chair and shrugged his shoulders. "Well, let's start with why there was a swarm of policemen shooting at me."

Miguel answered in a sarcastic tone, "Oh, you mean the eight policemen and the Federal Agent you murdered ... and how their families are never going to see them again?"

The cloaked man sat silent for a moment, staring at Miguel. Then he leaned forward and spoke. "Eight policemen performing an unauthorized sweep on a man you promised protection to and the Federal agent that led them! They stormed in on me with full intent to kill me. I think they call that pre-meditated murder."

"They were all officers of the law doing their job! My partner died in that blast! You're just twisting things around to make yourself appear innocent."

The cloaked man chuckled and stood up. "Innocent? None of us are innocent, Agent Perez, and, as for twisting things around, I wonder what excuse they would have given for being there. And if I remember correctly, one of your partner's men was trying to kill you before I arrived."

Miguel pondered that for a moment. Burk *was* trying to kill him … but why would he want to kill him?

The killer walked over to a small table that held a chessboard. It had a peculiar arrangement. On one side there was a full set of pieces, but on the other there was only one … a pawn with a miniature owl with its wings spread, perched proudly atop the piece.

"Do you play chess, Agent Perez?" the man asked as he analyzed the chessboard.

"What does that have to do with anything?" Miguel asked.

The killer turned towards Miguel. "I'll take that as a Yes. Personally, I never wanted to play until about seven years ago when the principle of the game became clear to me. You see, Miguel, chess is a game where everything revolves around rule-based strategy, where the pawns go first to soften the threat for the other pieces. The only problem I see with this game is that it reflects life. The pawns represent the everyday man, while the other pieces represent authority figures. What I'm trying to figure out is how can the pawn win without breaking the rules."

Miguel was somewhat puzzled at the killer's words although he knew what he was implying, so he decided to answer. "You can't win … the game isn't designed for the pawn to win."

The killer nodded and returned to his seat. "Precisely, Miguel, but once you take away the rules and allow the pawn to move as he pleases, things get interesting. The rest of the pieces have one of two choices … one, they can move out of the pawn's way … or two, they can suffer the consequences. Do you understand, Miguel?"

Miguel answered in a stern tone, "Yes, I understand! You're trying to say you are the pawn and have, for some reason, began targeting child predators and that the law enforcement agencies should stay out of your way. Am I right? I guess your next move is to use me as some sort of bargaining chip."

The cloaked man stood up and laughed. From under his coat he pulled out his Warthog knife and stood over Miguel. "Don't worry, Miguel, I'm not going to hurt you. I'm just going to pop these restraints I put on you for your own protection."

Miguel raised an eyebrow and spoke, "My protection?"

The killer eased the knife under the first restraint as he explained to Miguel why he had him tied down. "On your seat is a pressure switch that is attached to that ammo box under your chair. The box contains thirty-three pounds of high explosives. I wanted to make sure I had your complete attention while we have our little chat. This way you won't try something stupid."

Miguel chilled at the idea that there was a massive explosive device underneath him. He could not see it but he trusted it was there. "This guy is most likely a psychopath, but definitely not a stupid one," he thought to himself as he watched as the razor-sharp blade that had killed a fellow officer earlier pop the zip ties one-by-one.

The killer then walked over to a small table and picked up an ace bandage and pitched it to Miguel. "Here, Miguel. I would have done it myself, but I was afraid I would have gotten it too tight."

Miguel caught the bandage and painfully began wrapping it carefully around his aching ribcage.

"Let's get down to business, shall we?" the killer said as he walked to a wall on Miguel's left that was covered by a long tarp. The cloaked man reached for the tarp and pulled it down, revealing a massive collage of missing children posters.

Miguel looked on as the man silently walked down the wall, gazing at the pictures as if searching for some hidden message. Then he stopped and began to speak, "I'm sure you thought I was ready to turn myself over to you when I agreed to talk to you a few days ago, but that's not the reason I brought you here. You and I, Agent Perez, are linked and it's time you found out how. You may not like what I have to say … or even believe me at all, but I assure you I have no intention of turning myself in."

"What link? And what does a wall full of kids' pictures have to do with piling up victims in motel rooms?" Miguel asked.

The cloaked man walked back to his seat and lit a cigarette. "Let me start from the beginning … that seems the best way for you to understand."

Miguel listened as the man began to tell the story of his first victim, the first in a long, bloody trail that claimed the lives of over 600 victims in the last seven years.

Chapter 4

▼

Suffer The Children

December 3rd, 2000–8:30 pm

The almost silent tapping of fingers softly echoed through a small motel room in Tyler, Texas. A computer screen produced seemingly endless lines of messages that reflected in the eyes of the silent man at the keyboard.

This was a test. A few months earlier the cloaked man had heard of child predators luring children in via Internet chatrooms such as the one on his monitor now. He suspected this website in particular, named "Uptown Girl", was littered with child predators that hunt like animals, preying upon gullible children to fulfill their sexual deviances. Unfortunately for them, tonight another hunter was searching the chatroom disguised as a young girl with a curiosity for older men.

The first two hours turned up nothing. Then, as he was about to give up, a message popped up. A subscriber named "Supersexy" had asked the supposed young girl for a private chat. The cloaked man narrowed his eyes, typed in a positive response, and began to exchange messages with Supersexy.

After about thirty minutes, the inevitable happened. The man sent a picture of himself and asked to meet his intended victim. The cloaked man replied that he was a shy girl and only thirteen. Supersexy answered by saying it did not bother him and he had to meet her. Reading this, the cloaked man agreed to meet and responded with an address where they could meet. All he had to do now was wait.

He leaned back in the chair with a creak and collected his thoughts. It had been only a few months since he had lost his family, but the pain stung him as if it were only yesterday. He thought of the house he had bought for them. It was a simple house, painted red and surrounded by a quiet meadow. He had spent the preceding month filling it with the necessities before their arrival. He would have finally been happy ... but all of that had changed with the pull of a trigger.

He recalled the week after their death. He remembered standing in front of the empty house and how he set fire to it, watching it crumble like the rest of his dreams. That night would be with him forever. It was the moment that he had shed himself of hope, replacing it with only the will to inflict pain on those responsible for the deaths of his new wife and child. Like the fire that consumed the red house, his hatred began to burn away all that was left of his soul.

Something else changed that night. Every time after he passed a graveyard or a missing poster on a wall, he could hear whispering. At first he could not decipher the words but, as the days passed by, the voices became clear. They were the voices of children ... children whose cries for help had led him to this motel room.

The cloaked man shook the memories out of his head and looked at the clock. He wondered how long it would take, or if the man would show up at all. Either way, he was prepared to take his life. With his left hand he reached into a suitcase and pulled out a silenced .45 automatic and moved it into the light. He pulled back the slide and loaded it with a snap of the action. He rested the cool side of the pistol on his face and closed his eyes, falling into a deep sleep.

His eyes popped open to a blinding flash of light. He raised his arm to shield his face from the painful brightness, only to realize that he was standing in a green field that stretched on seemingly forever. He turned his head, noticing that the terrain was completely flat, void of hills and trees. "Where the hell am I?" he muttered.

Suddenly, a loud boom rang out in the distance. He whipped his head in the direction of the sound and spotted two figures. He began to walk towards the two figures. As he drew close, their faces came into view. His eyes widened as he recognized them.

"Mayella! Isabel!" he yelled as he ran towards their smiling faces.

Suddenly, his moment of happiness turned to horror. Their faces, contorted with pain, cried out, holding their outstretched arms towards the running man, pleading for his help.

His tear-filled eyes watched helplessly as their bodies fell to the ground, torn and battered from the wounds they had received on the day of their deaths. The crying man ran to catch their falling bodies, pulling them to his chest. He looked at their pale, lifeless faces and began to howl in wretched pain as he fell to his knees rocking them back and forth.

He looked into the clear skies and bellowed with a scorching anger at the heavens, "*Why them ... they did nothing to deserve this*! If you wanted someone to die, why didn't you just take me! You heartless bastard!"

Suddenly the earth began to shake beneath him and the cloudless sky quickly filled with angry greenish clouds that churned with bolts of lightning. A cold gust of wind blew against him as he narrowed his fiery eyes at the darkening sky. He gently laid the bodies of the two women on the ground and softly brushed the hair from their silent faces.

"Forgive me," he whispered, rising to his feet with his fists clenched. His teeth were bared like that of a snarling dog as he raised his hand and pointed to the sky. "Do you think I am afraid of you? Go ahead! *Strike me down*! At least then I can be with them! You coward!"

A paralyzing bolt of lightning shot from the boiling clouds, engulfing him in a blanket of electricity. Then, like a shot, the bolt pulled him into the sky with incredible speed. He watched the ground below disappear as he was pulled through the violent storm, higher and higher.

For a moment everything was silent as he floated in mid air, bound by the glowing electricity. He looked straight ahead at a golden cloud in front of him that slowly opened, revealing a bright light that shone into his eyes. He cringed, blinking as he saw a robed figure whose head was the source of the white light.

He tried to speak but his mouth would not open as he watched the robed figure hold out a finger and speak in a thundering voice, "I need you to listen! My children suffer! The time has come for you to make amends for your wrongdoings. Destroy those that would harm them and maybe I will allow you to see your family again."

The words echoed around him as he noticed now that he was surrounded by dozens of translucent forms. Their whispering voices became louder as they drew closer to him, pelting his ears with the chaotic noise. He closed his eyes and clinched his teeth as the whispering voices swirled around him like a tornado.

Suddenly the voices stopped as if they were never there ... leaving only the sound of the rushing wind in his ears.

He opened his eyes slowly to a familiar, but unwelcome sight. A large white owl soared in the air directly in front of him. The bird of prey's large round eyes were filled with a flame-like glow that chilled him to the bone. The bird flapped its large, heavy wings and rushed past him causing a mighty gust of wind that sent him face-first back to the earth below.

The wind raced over his body as he plummeted faster and faster towards the grassy field below. The cloaked man's fear-stricken face grew wide as he opened his mouth, letting out a blood-curdling cry. Then, there was only blackness.

The cloaked man jolted in his seat and opened his eyes wildly, looking about the motel room. With a deep breath he steadied himself and placed his hands over his face at the vivid nightmare that had plagued his sleep. "I'm losing it," he muttered to himself.

A bright light shone through the curtains illuminating the killer's cat-like eyes. He silently got out of his chair to take his place behind the door ... to await his victim.

Donny Crippin, aka "Supersexy", once a small time coke dealer from Riverside, California, stepped out of his red 1967 Camaro and began to walk along the motel walkway, looking for the room number that would lead him to a young girl who could momentarily satisfy his predatory mental illness.

Donny has always had a taste for young girls ... really young. At the age of 16, he had been caught molesting a nine-year-old girl and sentenced to a juvenile detention center for the remainder of his youth. There, he learned quickly about the drug trade from various youthful gang members.

Once released, he began to practice his new-found source of income in his small California hometown and quickly found an endless supply of young girls, who he hooked on his powdered poison and manipulated like puppets ... fulfilling all of his sick needs.

June 18th, 1992

Donny had been sitting in his living room watching television. He had just loaded a pipe full of cocaine when he spotted a beautiful girl walking in front of his window to the house next door. Donny stopped the task at hand and peered out from the curtains, noticing that she and her parents were moving into the house next door. A smile crept across his face as the wheels in his sick mind began to turn ... developing a plan.

Being a good neighbor, Donny conversed with the family on a daily basis. He discovered that the couple used cocaine socially, which Donny gladly began to feed them for free, slowly luring them into his trap. Within a few months the couple was hopelessly addicted to the drug and had no clue what the man next door was doing with their daughter, now firmly in Donny's grasp.

As with most child predators, Donny soon became bored with the girl and decided it was time to move on. Those plans came to a grinding halt as the thirteen-year-old girl informed him that she was pregnant.

Donny panicked at the news. The thought of going to prison plagued him like a cancer that would not go away. He had to think of a way to get out of the predicament he was in. For days he racked his brain until he finally came up with a solution.

Donny walked to the house of the marked family, holding a small baggie of cocaine that he had laced with strychnine. He had never murdered anyone before but this had to be done. Once inside the home, the trio needed little persuasion as they filled a glass pipe with the tainted powder and began to smoke it, passing the instrument from one to the other.

Making an excuse to leave, Donny grabbed his pockets and told them he had forgotten the other bag at his house and would get it. He stood up and walked out of the door, never looking back as he stepped into his car and drove away, leaving the family to their demise.

The morning sun slowly crept through the quiet streets of the small Riverside neighborhood. The warm, bright rays climbed the wall of a small wooden-framed house, shining through the window into the lifeless eyes of the three figures that lay on the living room floor. At one time they were a happy family, full of hopes and dreams with a bright future. Now they lay dead ... the victims of a cold-hearted, pathetic monster.

Donny had a smile on his face as he drove into the city of Tyler, Texas, with a refreshed feeling. Rid of the problem that lay far behind him in California, his mind teemed with the idea that once he settled in his new environment, he could start over and exploit the drug scene and young girls here to his advantage. He had already made a few phone calls that landed him a job with the Mexican Mafia, who had a strong foothold in the local drug market. This was going to be a paradise.

December 3rd, 2000–10:15 pm

The cloaked man raised his head and pulled out the silenced .45 as a knock came at the door. He raised a voice changer to his mouth that altered the sound of his voice to that of a young woman's.

Donny clicked the door open and poked his head inside. "Hello, is anyone here?"

A voice came from inside the room that made him smile. "Come in. I'm in the shower."

Donny smiled as he walked inside and strolled into the bathroom, only to see that no one was in the empty stall. "What the hell?" he thought to himself as he turned to find a large, dark man blocking his way out. The unexpected giant squeezed the trigger of his .45, sending a slug into Donny's forehead. Donny stumbled backwards, uttering a low moan as his life drained from him. The room began to spin as he weaved and fell flat-faced on the carpet.

A chuckle came from the killer as he lowered his weapon and walked over to the dying man on the floor. He quickly searched through Donny's pockets and pulled out his wallet, finding a thick wad of cash and a handful of credit cards. He shoved the pedophile's loot into one of the gray trench coat's large pockets.

The killer had reached down, grabbing Donny's leg to pull him between the wall and the bed, when the sound of his laptop beeping took his attention. He looked curiously at the screen and walked over to the computer. He couldn't believe his eyes. There were at least a dozen messages from what appeared to be more perverted chatroom stalkers, all wanting to meet the non-existent girl on the other end.

"Jesus," he muttered under his breath as he pulled Donny's lifeless body into the corner. Then he returned to the desk and began typing.

The experiment had worked like a charm. Like moths to a flame they came in one by one and like a hungry spider, the cloaked figure took their lives from them. By the end of the night he had taken eight of them, pocketing over 5000 dollars in cash and at least three dozen credit cards.

He looked at the pile of money when an idea hit him. He could not help but smile as he realized he had now found a way to finance a long-awaited revenge against those responsible for the deaths of his family and best friend.

A few months ago he was afraid of them. Their positions and strength made them seem invulnerable, but now he had seen that he could be just as vicious and brutal as they were. He now saw the path in front of him clearly. A path filled with blood, and he had taken the first step. The time had come.

The cloaked man packed up his gear and opened the door carefully, scanning the parking lot. He quickly stepped out and briskly walked along the walkway to his vehicle. As he passed the now deceased Donny Crippin's red Camaro, a young man stood up from the side of the car and spoke. "Hey, Sir. Does this car belong to you?"

The cloaked man nodded his head, noticing a camera in the boy's hand.

"Do you mind if I take a picture of it, Sir? I've always wanted a Camaro like this since I was little."

The cloaked man shook his head and replied, "No … no picture."

The young man hung his head and began walking away, across the parking lot. The cloaked man smiled to himself as he pulled out a keychain that read "Camaro". He opened the car's door and searched the glove box, finding the car's title. His eyes turned to the console where a pen lay. He smiled again and grabbed it as he exited the car. "Hey kid! Come here for a minute."

The young man quickly turned and almost tripped over himself as he made his way back across the parking lot. He noticed that the man was wearing an outfit that looked much like the Invisible Man. A gray fedora, gray trench coat, and a white wrapping that covered the bottom half of his face. The way the man was dressed seemed odd but he shrugged it off. After all, it was freezing outside and the man might be cold-natured.

The killer spoke while he wrote on the title, "Where are you going this early in the morning, son?"

The young man replied, "I'm going to work. Please, can I take a picture of the Camaro, Sir?" he asked again. "My job is a few miles from here and I don't have a lot of time."

The cloaked man chuckled and said, "I told you already, no pictures. By the way, what's your name?"

The young man sighed and replied, "James Crane, Sir."

"Well, James Crane, this is your lucky day. All I ask is that you get some insurance and take care of it." With that he handed the title and the keys to the youth.

The boy's mouth dropped as he stared in disbelief at what had just happened. "Are you sure, Sir? I mean this is a nice car … and uhh …"

The cloaked man laughed and shook his head at the boy's confusion. "You had better hurry or you'll be late for work."

The young man's face lit up into a huge smile as he stepped into the car and cranked it. He leaned out of the window to thank the man as he eased out of the parking lot, but he was gone. "Thanks, anyway!" he yelled as he hit the accelerator hard, smoking the tires as he sped down the highway.

The cloaked man smiled under his veil as he walked behind the building and stepped into his black van. With his right hand he picked up a week-old newspaper he had saved. The front page read "Cult Leader Acquitted". As he had done all week, he stared at the photo of the grinning man walking out of the courthouse, then at the two Federal agents that stood at the top of the steps. His eyes narrowed and focused on the young Mexican agent, reading his name.

"Miguel Perez, it has to be you. Let's see what you are made of."

Chapter 5

Motives Revealed

Miguel sat in silence as the man finished the story and then gave his assessment in a sarcastic tone. "Do you really expect me to buy that crap? That dead children speak to you and tell you to murder and rob innocent men? You're insane!"

A rage flew over the cloaked man as he leapt out of his chair and snatched Miguel by the throat. "A petty thief murdering innocent men! Innocent! Look at that wall, Miguel! *Look at it*!" he shouted.

"I don't know what you see, but I see a wall of despair. A wall of young lives that were stamped out by these victims of society you protect with your damn laws and political rules. Do you see those faces, Miguel? *They* are innocent and, as long I draw breath, I will do everything I can to stop more of them from ending up on those damn posters."

With that, he shoved Miguel's head back and walked across the room to calm himself. The cloaked man turned back to Miguel, speaking in a harsh voice, "If I remember correctly, I'm not the only one in this room that has murdered someone."

Miguel gasped for air as he recovered from the man's iron grip. He knew that his taunting would get a reaction but he was not expecting it to be that violent. He looked at the man who paced like a wounded animal. He was making some headway with him but he would have to choose his words carefully from here on out. He could tell that the cloaked man did not want to hurt him, but he was definitely unstable.

"You had a child, didn't you? What happened?" Miguel asked.

The cloaked man leaned against the wall and raised his eyes to Miguel, "You knew her. You were there. You saw what they did."

Miguel was puzzled at the man's answer. "I'm sorry, I don't know what you're talking about? I've handled a lot of cases where children were murdered and I try to forget about them."

The killer turned and walked back to the chair, rubbing his veiled chin in thought. "I'm sure you will remember this one. It was a turning point for you, as it was for me. Just like your first case. You remember? The one you lost? What was his name?"

Miguel replied, "Tartin? How did you know about that?"

The cloaked man chuckled and spoke as he sat down in the chair, "How did I know? I've been watching you for a long time, Miguel. Yes, the good Reverend Tartin and his mindless followers … sick people. Shall I tell you how they died?"

Miguel felt a cold chill. How long had this man been hiding in the shadows? How much did he know about him? One thing was for sure, he had been planning this meeting for quite some time and he was leading up to something bigger than the confession of crime.

December 3rd, 2000

The Reverend Jim Tartin walked out of the Provo, Utah, courthouse a free man. Tartin, the leader of a fanatical cult that was a mixture of Islam and ancient Celtic rituals, had been accused of murdering a young child that was found dismembered and drained of blood a few miles from his mountaintop compound.

Two months prior he had been arrested for the girl's murder by a promising young FBI agent named Miguel Perez. His first case, Perez had meticulously combed through the evidence. Everything pointed to the cult … from the tire tread pattern found on Tartin's car to fingerprints that matched several of his cult members.

During the murder investigation, Perez learned that Tartin formed his cult in the late 70's and had remained quiet until recently when the eccentric leader began slipping into drug-induced stupors and having visions he interpreted as omens that the end of the world was near. Lately, he and his group had become more withdrawn, rarely leaving the compound.

In court, the Reverend had an ace up his sleeve. That ace was attorney Douglas Banks. Rookie agent Perez and his veteran partner, Larry Jones, sat dismayed in the cold courtroom as the defendant's attorney shredded their case in front of their eyes. In any other courtroom the mounting evidence would have easily been enough to convict someone of this crime, but Bank's eloquent speaking abilities and vast knowledge of the law painted Tartin to be a victim of governmental harassment because of his religious beliefs.

"We're going to lose this one," Miguel muttered to Jones, who nodded and leaned over to his partner.

"This guy is guilty as sin ... you can see it in his eyes. I've seen Banks at work before. He once defended this big-time gangbanger in Dallas who worked for the "13" drug cartel. This punk had a customer who owed him 500 bucks. He skinned the man's wife and two daughters alive to send him a collection reminder. Fortunately, the youngest daughter lived long enough to ID the attacker. Long story short, Bank's got him off. Funny thing happened to the dealer though. They found him in a dumpster in Oak Cliff. He'd been beaten beyond recognition and his throat was cut. Poetic justice, huh?"

Miguel shook his head. "I guess the women's family found him."

Larry looked at Miguel and whispered again, "That's the weird part of the whole thing. The father was the only surviving family member and he shot himself a week after the coke dealer skinned his family. They just found the dealer in the dumpster yesterday."

Miguel was about to reply when the judge called a recess for jury deliberations. Miguel stood and turned to his partner. "Well, I suppose this is it. I hope this jury isn't blind." Three hours later the two agents stood on the courthouse steps and watched Banks and Tartin walk out like POWs stepping off the Freedom Flight.

"That bastard. He's going to do it again. I know he will!" the younger agent angrily predicted.

Larry placed his hand on Miguel's shoulder and tried to reassure his partner. "The Bureau will be watching him from here on out. If he screws up again, we'll get him."

Miguel looked at his partner and replied, "Yeah, I know, Larry, but that means someone else will have to die. Damn, I wish there was someone who could take this guy out." The two watched as the victorious attorney and his client drove away in a limousine, waving to the press that had gathered for the trial.

Larry shoved his hands in his pockets and turned to his frustrated partner. "I suppose we need to get to the airport. Our flight leaves in an hour."

Miguel turned with a puzzled look. "An hour? When did you make reservations?"

Larry smiled, "I made reservations yesterday. This trial was over before it began. When you've been doing this as long as I have, you'll know when you're beaten. Don't worry, you've got plenty of time … the world is full of criminals."

Chapter 6

Intervening Divinity

December 4th, 2000

The late evening sun was setting on the compound as Tartin looked out from his bedroom window at the glorious sight when a knock came at his door.

"Come in," he said as a young woman walked in with her head down. "How can I help you, my child?" the Reverend asked softly as he walked over and began to rub her shoulders. The young woman raised her eyes with a pained look on her face.

"I know you said Sheena must be sacrificed for the good of the flock, but I can't help feeling guilty about it."

The Reverend lifted the woman's chin with his finger and gently kissed her forehead. "Do not worry, my child. It will pass in time. God has told me that you should feel no guilt and you must trust me as God does."

Tartin began to undress the woman and laid her in his bed. He smiled and whispered in her ear as he penetrated her beautiful young body. He could not help but feel a bit evil at the power that he exercised over his followers. With a word they would do anything for him, especially sexual in nature, and he took advantage of their loyalty over and over again … both men and women, and sometimes their children. To their brainwashed minds, it was a blessing for him to take them to his bed. In the Reverend's mind, he was God.

A silent figure slipped through the wire fence of the compound and vanished into the shadows like a black cat hunting its prey. With scanning eyes and steady hands, he slowly raised a scoped Jennings Devastator crossbow to his shoulder and took aim at a large man that was patrolling the courtyard carrying a MAC-10 machine pistol.

He continued to survey the dark compound and noticed three more guards, all armed the same. He chuckled to himself as he sighted in the nearest guard and clicked off the safety.

"Lots of hardware for a church group," he thought to himself as he squeezed the trigger and sent the razor-tipped bolt sizzling across the courtyard and through the neck of the guard, a large chunk of shattered bone and blood exploding out of the gaping wound.

The hulking man reeled, grabbing his perforated throat as a massive river of hot blood gushed from his throat and splattered onto the frozen ground at his feet. The guard then dropped to his knees and fell backwards hard on the ground, a geyser of steam rising from the hole in his neck.

The killer quickly reloaded and took aim at a second guard. He did not know for sure, but it was an almost certainty that most, if not all, of these religious fanatics were armed. He must get in closer. One by one, the guards fell victim to the crossbow's deadly bolts as they thudded onto the icy ground.

Once they were silenced, he crept over to the nearest lifeless guard and retrieved the MAC-10 and extra magazines. He checked the weapon as he slipped in the back door to one of the sleeping areas in the compound.

"Just like shooting fish in a barrel," he muttered, raising the dead guard's weapon at the group of Tartin's followers that were intertwined, orgy-like on the floor.

The MAC-10 rythmed like a sewing machine as it pelted the men and women in a fiery hail of lead. They cried out in anguish as the slugs ripped through their bodies, spattering blood on the far wall. He quickly reloaded and fired another volley into any survivors, silencing their pleas for help.

Suddenly, a door to his left opened and a man with a shouldered weapon stepped through. Without thinking, he wheeled towards the man and emptied the magazine into his body, sending him flying backwards into the main house. A click from the open bolt sounded as he ran out of ammunition. He dropped the empty MAC-10 to the ground and pulled his Franchi SPAS-15 from under his trench coat.

In a series of quick strides, he stepped over the dead guard and made his way down the long hallway that led deeper into the main house. A guard hearing the gunfire and screams turned a corner of the hallway, chambered a round into his weapon and came face to face with the cloaked figure. Surprise turned to fear as he raised his assault rifle, only to be cut nearly in half by the massive shotgun blast that slammed him against the wall.

Upstairs, Tartin was interrupted from his sexual activity as the thunderous blast of the shotgun caught his attention. His door flew open and a member of his flock ran in with a panicked look on his face.

"*What's going on out there?*" Tartin screamed.

"He's shooting us! *He's killing everyone!*" came the hysterical reply.

A volley of automatic gunfire came from downstairs as the remaining cult members battled with the phantom. Trails of armor-piercing slugs penetrated the walls, some finding their mark in the confused, screaming cult members.

Tartin grabbed a pistol from under his pillow and buckled up a Kevlar vest.

The young man standing in the door of Tartin's quarters shouted, "*There he is!*" as he raised his weapon and fired toward the dark, vast living room. Tartin watched in horror as a series of thundering shotgun rounds blasted the young man, sending pieces of his body flying into the room. A groan came from the squirming boy as the stunned Tartin heard the sound of boots clicking on the hardwood floor, moving towards his bedroom.

Tartin raised his Glock 40 and traced the audible steps as they moved down the hall just outside the room. With a loud curse, he emptied the pistol in a line along the wall in hopes of hitting the approaching killer. The smell of gunpowder flooded his heavily breathing nostrils as he listened for any sign of life outside.

His pistol emptied, he reached into his nightstand and fumbled with a full magazine, dropping it on the floor. He dropped to his knees and reached for the clip as the killer entered the door. The cult leader was horrified as he stared down the barrel of the long, black shotgun. His eyes met the gaze of the cloaked man whose staring eyes seemed to be filled with flames as he chambered a round into his weapon.

"I have money! Lots of it! Over … over there in that safe! Just please, please don't kill me!" the Reverend begged as, leaving the fresh magazine on the floor as he stood.

The specter-like man remained silent as he reached into his pocket and produced a newspaper, throwing it at the shaking man's feet. Tartin glanced down at the photo of the young girl on the front page, then back to the man's narrowed, glowing eyes.

"Her name was Sheena Weston and she was only four years old. I want you to remember this child as you burn in Hell," the deadly intruder broke his silence.

Tartin quivered in fear as he backed up against the bed and sternly pointed a finger at the killer.

"If you harm me, God will strike you down! I am Jim Tartin! I am the New Messiah! And you will pay for this sacrilege!"

The killer laughed at the feeble taunt.

"We all have sins to pay for." With a powerful thrust, he slammed the steel collapsible stock into Tartin's head, knocking him out cold on the floor.

"I'll deal with you in a minute, Reverend."

Leaning the shotgun on the wall momentarily, the cloaked man turned his attention to the safe in the corner. Taking out 2 small packages that he carried in a pocket of his trench coat, he carefully unrolls the contents of one of the packages into a long, thin line. Peeling the protective tape from the adhesive-backed explosive strip, he adheres the C-4 to the hinge side of the steel box. He then laid the second package atop the safe and inserted its wire leads into the mounted charge. The killer flipped the arming toggle, and quickly stepped out of harm's way as the short delay of the small but powerful device expires, blowing the safe door loose.

He stepped back to the partially open safe door, grabbing the exposed hinge side with his strong, gloved hands and pulls the door free. He quickly transferred the large stacks of cash into a collapsible canvas bag pulled from his trench coat.

Suddenly, a noise from under the bed caused him to wheel around and unholster his .45 automatic. Crawling from under Tartin's bed, the young naked woman scrambled to her feet and ran screaming out of the bedroom door and into the hallway. She looked behind her in time to see the cloaked man exiting Tartin's room and taking aim. He jerked the trigger, sending the full metal jacket bullet screaming after the fleeing woman. The bullet caught her just above the kidney, knocking her across the hardwood floor.

Seeing that his target had fallen, he clenched his teeth and quickly walked over to the woman who was helplessly crawling towards the stairway. He reached down, grabbing her ankle with his thick, leaded glove and jerked her into the air, flipping her on her back. He raised the pistol, aimed it at her forehead. His eyes cringed and narrowed as he recognized her face.

"I know who you are. You're the mother of the murdered child. How could you allow this to happen?"

The woman coughed as a bubble of blood filled her mouth, then turned her head away from the question. The cloaked man's eyes filled with rage at her silence.

"*Answer me!*" he shouted as he kicked her in the side with his flat-nosed boot. The woman cried out from the blow and looked at her attacker.

"*We had to!* It was the only way! God required it. Her blood had to be shed."

The cloaked man stepped back on hearing her words and closed his eyes. He could not fathom that anyone could be so cruel, so uncaring. He almost felt sorry for her as he knelt down and turned her face to his. He slowly pulled down his veil, exposing his face.

The young woman looked up at him. Her eyes widened with fear as she noticed the scar on the right side of his face.

"You are him! I saw it in my dreams. The White Owl, you have his mark. The Owl said you would have mercy if I told you."

The killer was stunned by her words. He paused for a moment.

"If you told me what?"

The young girl pointed to a door at the far end of the hall.

"There is where he keeps the children. In that room. Please have mercy on me. The Owl promised."

The killer rose and aimed the pistol at her forehead.

"The Owl promised you too much."

The gun jerked as the .45 slug blew the back of her head over the wooden floor. He pulled the veil over his face and walked to the door the woman had pointed to. With a heavy kick, he smashed the door in and entered the room with the shotgun readied. In front of him were about 15 children. Innocent eyes looked at him with fear as he stepped into the light. He glanced down at the shotgun and quickly lowered it as he approached the frightened children.

"It's ok. Don't be scared. I'm going to get you out of here."

The children remained silent as he knelt down and beckoned the children to go with him.

"I need you to follow me, ok? I need you to hold hands and close your eyes."

One of the children tried to speak but only an unintelligible sound came out. Tears welled up in the clocked man's eyes as a sight hit him that chilled him to the bone. All the children had their tongues removed.

The children held hands as he led them out of the house, making sure they did not see the dead that lay strewn about inside the compound. Once in the yard, he looked around and spotted a bus that the cult occasionally used to bring in new members. He led the children to it and opened the vehicle's door.

"Stay in here and keep your heads down. I'll be back in a minute."

He closed the bus door and returned to the main house, his mind filling with rage as he entered the bedroom where the moaning Tartin was just beginning to regain consciousness. He snatched Tartin off the ground and slammed him against the wall.

"You sick son of a bitch! You like hurting children?"

The Reverend Tartin's eyes were wide with fear as the cloaked man punched him over and over in the ribs with the leaded gloves, snapping his ribs with every blow. As Tartin screamed from the beating, the avenger reached into the shaking Reverend's mouth and grabbed his tongue. With a heave, he ripped it out and flung the detached body part, letting Tartin fall bleeding and writhing to the floor. The killer grabbed Tartin's leg and dragged the insane religious leader downstairs into the main room where he handcuffed him to a stair post.

The half-dead leader watched in horror as the man pulled dead cult members, one-by-one, into the large living room, then walked out of the house and came back with two large cans marked "Diesel". The cloaked man opened the containers and sloshed the flammable liquid on the bodies and walls of the large room. The remainder of the diesel he poured over the cowering Tartin's head.

He tossed the empty cans down, knelt and looked into Tartin's whimpering, bloody face.

"Not doing too well are you, Rev? Don't have anything to say, do ya? Well, I do. Tonight you are going to die a horrible death. If you are really the Messiah, you shouldn't have anything to worry about, but I have a feeling I will be seeing you in Hell. By the way, thanks for the money ... I'll put it to good use."

The killer moved to a phone on the wall and dialed 911. He spoke in a frantic voice as the operator answered. "Yes, this is Jim Tartin! I ... I need help! God told me to! God told me to kill! Please hurry! The children are outside! *Please hurry!*"

He dropped the phone and walked to the door. From a pocket in his trench coat he produced a Zippo lighter and, with a flick, the flame shot out of the steel case.

Tartin's terror-filled eyes watched as the man lit a cigarette and tossed the lighter on the floor, igniting the slow burning fuel. The killer tipped his hat at the squirming cult leader and walked out of the door towards the front gate as the orange flames grew higher and higher behind him. He broke into a smile as he heard Tartin screaming in intense pain from the fire that was consuming him.

"A little prelude of Hell for the good Reverend!" he muttered.

"The children," he thought to himself as he turned towards the bus. The eyes of the children were watching him as he stood there for a moment, wondering if he should leave them there alone. He saddened as the thought of their uncertain future ran through his mind. They would probably never recover from this ordeal.

He had taken a step towards the bus when the sound of sirens in the distance caught his attention. As the flashing lights drew closer, he commented, "Here comes the Calvary! Turning once more to look at the children, he reluctantly picked up the bag full of weapons and money and slipped into the night.

December 6th, 2000

Perez and Jones returned to their Dallas office to begin working on the mountain of paperwork that awaited them. They had no more stepped inside the door when the voice of Director Rafael Galvan rang out from behind them.

"Hey, ladies. I like how you screwed up that case in Utah. I should kick your asses but I need you to take another case. Follow me."

The two agents looked at each other in bewilderment as they entered Rafael's office. They had gotten off with only a slight mention of losing the Tartin case, a case that had taken months of hard work and resources.

"Director Galvan?" Miguel said humbly.

"I'm not complaining, but why aren't you jumping our asses like you usually do. We lost the case, Sir."

Rafael looked up and smiled as he sat an evidence box on his desk. "What! You two didn't hear?"

Miguel shrugged his shoulders. "Hear what, Sir?"

Rafael scratched the back of his head and laughed. "Your cult leader. Two days ago he went nuts and killed everyone in the house, including himself. He had called 911 and told them to hurry … that he was going to hurt the children. By the time they got there all that was left was ashes."

Larry spoke up, "What about the children?"

Rafael pulled out his chair, sat down and answered, "Safe and sound inside a bus at the compound. Bad thing was they had their tongues cut out. Sick bastards! Why would they do something like that? Anyway, it was ruled a mass suicide."

Larry looked at Miguel and smiled, "Looks like your wish came true."

Rafael cut their conversation short with his usual get-down-to-business demeanor. He patted the cardboard box on his desk and began to summarize the case.

"Larry, I know you remember Agent Servin, don't you?"

Larry nodded.

"Good. He resigned yesterday and I need you two to take over his case."

Larry, puzzled at the news, questioned, "Why did he resign?"

Rafael leaned back in his chair and answered, "He flipped out. He spent all day at the motel crime scene and later attended a press conference. Then yesterday, around noon, he called in his verbal resignation and checks into a mental hospital down in Rusk."

Miguel dug out Servin's case folder containing crime scene photos. A stack of bodies lay piled up between the wall and bed in what appeared to be a motel room. "When did this happen?" he asked.

Rafael held up another folder. "That happened three days ago in Tyler. These were taken at noon today in El Paso," he explained as he handed Miguel the second folder.

Miguel held up the two pictures and analyzed them. "Serial killer?" he questioned.

"Maybe? Maybe not." Rafael replied. "That's why I want you two on it. You're quick ... and we need answers before the media picks up on this. Now get to work."

The two agents carried the box into their office and began to sort through the evidence.

Miguel spoke as he looked at the stack of evidence photos for both crimes. "What do you think, Larry? Can we catch this guy?"

Larry shook his head as Miguel handed the photos to him. "Don't know, it's too soon. But I have a bad feeling this is going to be a long one. Whoever did this is vicious. The first thing we need to do is go to El Paso and snoop around a little bit. Somebody has to know something about it."

The two agents grabbed their coats and headed out of the office, leaving for El Paso to begin the investigation.

Chapter 7

Painful Memories

As the cloaked man continued to talk, Miguel realized the man could not possibly be fabricating what he was hearing. He had too much factual information; he knew too many details that had never been released to the public. He needed to know more and began to question his captor.

"Why me? You mentioned earlier that I knew your daughter? How could I have possibly known her?"

The killer stood again and walked towards the wall of posters. He moved down the wall, hanging his head as if pondering the best way to answer. He stopped and slowly lifted his head.

"First, I need you to look at something. Do you mind?"

He pulled out an old photograph and carefully handed it to Miguel. There were three people in the picture. A young girl, maybe four or five, grinned widely at the camera and a pleasant looking woman smiled beside her. A scar ran down the left side the woman's face. Standing behind them was a tall, longhaired man with the two females wrapped up in his long, thick arms.

Miguel's eyes moved back to the woman. She looked so familiar. Where did he know her from?

The cloaked man took a step toward him and asked, "Do you remember why you left the Customs Agency, Miguel?"

The agent squinted his eyes at the question, then looked back at the picture. "This was your daughter?"

The killer nodded and replied, "Yes, my step-daughter … but I always thought of her as my own. She was a light to my soul."

Miguel flipped the picture over and read the date on the back. "2-3-00" His eyes grew wide as it all began to make sense. His stomach turned as the little girl's face suddenly flashed from his memory. He looked up slowly at the towering killer that stood over him. It had to be a coincidence. That day, 2-3-00, the little girl and the longhaired man … he flipped the picture over again, remembering where he had seen this picture before.

He leaned back in his chair and closed his eyes as he recalled the terrible memory that had caused him years of nightmares, now playing vividly in his mind like an old film.

February 3rd, 2000

U.S. Customs Officer, Miguel Perez, sat quietly behind his desk at the border crossing station in Laredo, Texas. Although it was not the best job in the world, the pay was all right and it was a good reference for any future career possibilities. Most of the work was boring, but every now and then some excitement popped up … the usual college student trying to smuggle that extra bottle of liquor, or the elderly tourist with a huge prescription of Viagra, and, more recently, a noticeable increase in cocaine smugglers.

A new drug gang had risen to power in Nuevo Laredo that called themselves the "13". They were desperate to cross their poison into the United States. At first, their methods were basic, hiding the cocaine in clothes and bags. Then they evolved different methods such as stuffing their body orifices with coke-filled balloons.

Over the last month he had heard of more extreme, sick methods of smuggling employed by the vicious cartel, methods that included using animals and children to transport their drugs.

Miguel sat at his desk reading the morning paper when a commotion from one of the turnstile lines caught his attention. An extremely large man threw his arms up and began to argue with the customs officer working the line, causing the officer to back up at the outburst.

Miguel noticed that he was holding a suspicious looking red duffle bag tightly in his hand. He exited his office and approached the two arguing men. The angry man turned his head to the approaching agent and stared hard into his face. The look he gave Miguel made the hair stand up on the back of his neck, but he kept his composure and spoke sternly to the longhaired man. "Sir! Please come with me."

The man's eyes widened with surprise. "What the hell did I do now?"

Miguel narrowed his eyes and pointed towards his office. "Nothing yet, Sir. Will you please follow me?"

The man straightened his stance and nodded his head. "Ok ... I don't want any trouble."

Miguel took the red bag and led the man into the room. "Sit down over there, Sir."

The big man sat down quietly as Miguel began to examine the bag. He glanced at the nervous man. He was even bigger up close; his size and long hair resembled that of Chewbacca from Star Wars, yet he sat like a child in the principle's office, squirming on the seat and tapping his fingers. Miguel felt a bit sorry for the big man and decided to make small talk to ease his nervousness.

"What seemed to be the problem out there, Sir?"

The big man answered softly, "I couldn't find my license. I must have left it at home."

"Home?" Miguel continued, "You live in Mexico?"

"Yes, Sir." the big man nodded. "I have a wife and daughter down there. Well, a stepdaughter, but I think of her as my own."

Miguel noticed that the man seemed to be calming down as he felt something hard in the bag and pulled out a wallet. "Is this your wallet?"

The big man smiled with relief. "Yes. Yes, it is. My license should be in there."

Miguel opened the wallet and pulled out the man's license. A picture fell out on the counter and Miguel slowly picked it up. Three happy people stood smiling in front of a small apartment. He looked at the woman. She was beautiful, except for a scar that ran down the left side of her face. She looked so familiar, where had he seen her before?

His train of thought was broken by the big man's voice. "That's my family. We took that picture this morning. They're beautiful, aren't they?"

Miguel smiled and slid the picture back in the man's wallet. "I think that will be all. You are free to go. Just remember to keep your wallet handy from now on." He handed the red bag back to the longhaired man and escorted him out the office door. He watched as the man disappeared into the crowd.

Turning to walk back into his office, the sound of one of the Customs drug dogs caught his attention as it clawed and scratched at a woman holding a child wrapped in a Falsa blanket.

Everything seemed to be moving in slow motion as the woman threw the child down and tried to run out of the check station, only to be grabbed by a customs officer. Miguel sprinted over to the dog that was frantically clawing the motionless child. He grabbed the dog's collar, pulling back hard to get the dog off of the child. What he saw next would he would never forget, scarring him for the rest of his life.

As he pulled the dog backwards, one of its claws hung in the blanket, pulling it free. Miguel's face dropped as he stared at the lifeless child. Her abdomen had been sewn up with leather stitches. He began to shake as he knelt down and touched her cold face. Tears filled his eyes as he realized what had happened. He had heard rumors of this horrible act before … using children to transport drugs, but he had found it hard to believe. No one could be that inhuman, no one could do such a barbaric thing, but there it was in front of him. He looked around at the gawking crowd, and then to the cursing woman who was struggling to escape from the customs officer.

He reached down tenderly and pulled the little girl to his chest. His tears fell gently on her cheeks as he slowly raised his eyes towards the woman whose face was contorted with anger as she fought the customs agent trying to handcuff her. She cared nothing for the child in his arms, only that she had been caught.

His left hand reached to his side and slowly pulled his Springfield .45 automatic pistol from its holster. A rush of hatred raced through his veins as he brought the sights up, resting on the face of the evil human that stood before him.

"She doesn't deserve a trial!" he thought to himself as he pulled the trigger, releasing the solid copper hollow-point from the black steel barrel of the pistol. He could almost see the bullet as it struck the fighting woman in the neck, severing her spinal cord in a spray of blood and bone. The woman dropped her arms and teetered as her head folded to her chest. After what seemed like forever, her lifeless body thudded to the ground.

A feeling of satisfaction and relief filled Miguel for putting an end to the monster that lay twitching on the floor.

Suddenly, the room began to spin as the distress of re-living that day took its toll on him. He closed his eyes, almost losing consciousness.

As he regained his composure, Miguel looked across the room at the cloaked man. His face was clasped in his hands as he tried to fight back the tears of sadness that filled his eyes. He shook his head and tried to speak, but only a choked whimper came out. He fell to his knees and held his hands tightly over the fedora as he sobbed loudly, rocking back and forth.

Miguel could not believe his eyes. The heartless killer he had been arguing with only moments before had been reduced to a quivering child-like character as he recalled his daughter's death. Miguel felt a lump in his throat form as he asked softly, "What was her name?"

The emotional man raised his pain-filled eyes and answered, "Isabella. Her name was Isabella. That day was the last day they were going to have to spend in that hell-hole!"

Miguel looked at the picture again and then up to the man. Stumbling to his feet, the distraught killer walked over to a television in the far corner and leaned over it as if he were having trouble standing.

Miguel asked, "The mother, what happened to her?"

The killer's mind replayed the last few moments he had spent with his two beautiful ladies. He had Isabel in his arms. She had giggled loudly and pushed at his face as he bared his teeth and growled playfully. "The old bear is gonna get you, ahhh"

The words rang fresh in his ears as Mayella walked out of the apartment and laughed at his childish antics. "You two are crazy," she had said as she gently ran her hand across his face.

The young man's eyes softened at the touch of her warm hands. He kissed her on the cheek and sat Isabel down. "Daddy's got to go now, baby. I love you."

She hugged his leg and looked up at him with her wide grin. "I love you, too, Daddy."

Then, Ruben's car had slowly pulled into the drive of the family's small apartment in Nuevo Laredo. The hulking man stepped out of the car and held out his hand to greet his friend. "Hey, Oso! This is the day, huh?"

The man smiled as he shook Ruben's hand. "Yeah, it is. What time do I need to be there?"

Ruben looked at his watch. "I'll have them there around seven. Don't look so worried … you know they'll be safe with me."

The man nodded his head and looked into Ruben's smiling face. "You are the best friend I've ever had, Ruben. I owe you, dude."

Ruben replied, "You are a good man, Oso. God has given you a second chance. I am honored to help you.

"Hey, I almost forgot!" Ruben had said as he reached in his car and grabbed a Polaroid camera. "This is a Kodak moment, no?" He beckoned for the trio to move together as he raised the camera and laughed, "Say cheese!"

The family smiled as he took two pictures. He handed one to the young man. "This one is for you and the other is for me. Hey, you need me to help you lock up around here?"

The young man shook his head and replied, "No, that's ok. I have a few things to handle in town before I leave anyway."

Ruben nodded and clapped his hands together. "Ok then, I'll go ahead and take them to my house. I'll see you at seven tonight."

The young man turned to his wife, who was bright with excitement. He grabbed her hands and slid his fingers between hers, gripping them gently as he pulled her to him. "I'll see you tonight, Baby. I love you."

She reached up and kissed him gently. He had stared into her eyes and smiled as she spoke the words, "I love you, too, Mi Amore."

He put his arms around both of his "ladies" as he called them and closed his eyes. His dreams had finally come true. They were going home.

The killer's fists crackled in his leaded leather gloves as an uncontrollable rage filled his body. He yelled out loudly, smashing his hand through the screen of the television in a shower of sparks. Effortlessly, he flung the useless television across the room, crashing it against the wall.

His eyes glared with hatred as he roared like an angry bear, leaping to where the television lay on the floor. He began to kick and crush it as he tried to quell his anger. "The "13"! That's what happened to her! That's what happened to all of us! Two hours! Two more fucking hours and they would have been home, safe with me!"

As he calmed, the killer returned to his seat and sat with his head down. Then, as if his fit of rage had never happened, he began to speak, "Tell me something, Miguel. Why was your partner at that house … and who was the man that put a bullet in me?"

Miguel had momentarily pushed aside any thoughts of the failed raid on the farmhouse and his partner's death. As he recalled the events of that day, they made no sense.

"Why was he there? I honestly don't know. You and I had had agreed to meet and if something went wrong, I would call him. As for the man that shot you, I don't know who he was."

Hearing this, the killer reached into his pocket and produced a folder. Holding it out to Miguel, he said, "Maybe this will explain it. There's a lot about your dead partner that you don't know. Please, I insist."

Miguel opened the folder and began to read. His eyes could not believe what was laid out before him. His partner, a decorated Marine and FBI agent, was turning into no more than a drug-dealing murderer with every turn of the page.

He looked at the signature. Below every picture, receipt, and note was a familiar name. He raised his head and looked at the killer. "These are Agent Servin's notes! Where did you get these?"

The killer turned and spoke, "He gave them to me before he died."

January 1st, 2001

A tall, broad-shouldered man dressed in a doctor's lab coat entered the Cherokee County Mental Rehabilitation Facility in Rusk, Texas. His black dress shoes clicked on the marble-tiled floor of the old building as he made his way to the receptionist desk.

He spoke politely to the young lady behind the counter, "Excuse me, ma'am. I'm Doctor Joe Styles. I'm here to evaluate a Mr. Ybalde Servin."

The young girl smiled at the man and pulled the patient's file. "May I ask who this evaluation is for?"

The man smiled and answered, "I represent the Federal Bureau of Investigation. This is merely a routine evaluation. I can show you my credentials, if you'd like?"

The young woman looked at the evaluation roster and shook her head. "I don't see your appointment here, Doctor Styles."

The man rubbed his balding head. "Oh dear, I didn't call it in. I forgot how much things have changed since 9-11. I'm not quite used to the new protocol … I'll just come back later."

The secretary watched as the doctor closed his briefcase and turned to walk out. "Doctor Styles? Hold on. I believe I can help you. I'll write you in for an appointment. I just need you to sign off on it."

The tall man smiled and pulled a pen from his pocket. "Thank you, ma'am, this will only take a few minutes," he said, signing the form. "You've really helped me out. Where can I find Agent Servin?"

The secretary stepped from behind the counter and pointed towards a fountain. "There he is. He spends all day watching that fountain. I'm sure it won't hurt for you to talk to him."

The tall man fixed his eyes on an old, gray-haired man. "No ma'am, it won't hurt a bit."

The tranquil sound of the water fountain filled the tall man's ears as he sat down slowly on the bench beside the former agent who had faked insanity in order to resign from the Bureau.

The ex-federal agent swallowed hard as he looked over at the doctor, then back at the fountain.

"I knew it was you. The photo ... the note ... I knew you would come for me sooner or later." His eyes teared as he reached into his shirt pocket and pulled out a folded piece of paper.

"I was a different man back then ... greedy and ruthless. I should have never hired that animal. We had used children to transport drugs before, but we only drugged them. I didn't know he was going to kill the little girl or your wife, but I guess that doesn't matter now, does it?"

The killer sighed and looked at the ground. "I know you didn't, but you let it happen ... just like you turned your head when they shot Ruben. He was your son and he deserved better than that. They *all* deserved better."

The old man began to sob. "It all turned into a big mess. Carlos grabbed the child and the woman fought him. That's when Ruben came out. Carlos shot your wife and child and I stood there and did nothing. Then Carlos saw that damned picture ... the picture with your face. He went crazy. That's when Ruben ran for it. I ... I just stood there!"

The old man looked into the killer's eyes. "I know what you are here to do. Here ... these are directions to a house where I kept records of everything that went on. You'll find everything you need to know about the "13". But I must warn you, be careful with the 13's leader when you try to take him out ... he's a dangerous man and far from stupid. I hope you send him to Hell for what he has done to you and your family."

The killer reached into his white coat, and pulled out a small, greenish pill. "This is cyanide ... the same kind they issue to CIA agents. You seem like a changed man, Ybalde, and I appreciate your help. I'm sure God will forgive you, but I can't."

The old man gently took the capsule from the killer's palm and held it into view. He turned and smiled at the killer. "May I share something with you, Oso?"

The killer nodded his head, "Sure, go ahead."

The old man touched the killer's shoulder and stared hard into his eyes. "My father was a full-blooded Apache Shaman. He used to tell me the story of a White Owl that would come to visit you before your death. I dreamt of him last night. I knew then that judgment was coming for me ... and that you would have mercy. The White Owl flies with you, Oso, and I hope that one day you will be repaid all that is owed to you."

With that, Ybalde placed the capsule under his tongue. The poison worked quickly as it absorbed through the blood vessels in his mouth and into his body. The killer caught Ybalde's falling head and carefully rested it on his chest.

"Goodbye, Agent Servin," he whispered as he stood and walked away, leaving the remorseful man lifeless on the bench.

Miguel was in shock as he reached the end of the folder. He knew now why Larry was at the house. Larry was afraid that Servin would expose his involvement with the notorious "13" drug gang.

A startling thought hit him ... Burk's actions were no accident either. Although he was a loose cannon, he'd always obeyed Larry. That meant that his partner had wanted him dead.

Miguel turned to the last page. It was a list of names and addresses of everyone involved with the 13's drug trade. Servin had been very thorough in putting together this incriminating information. Photos and occupations were posted beside the major players. Sadly, he found the names and pictures of every one of Larry's team on the list. As he continued to scan the document, he recognized the photos of many men who had turned up dead over the past few years in unusual situations.

Miguel looked up slowly as another revelation came to him about the cloaked man. "You are not just killing child predators in motel rooms are you?" Miguel asked. "You're going after the "13" as well. My God! There must be 50 or 60 of these men that I know have been murdered in recent years. We thought it was a gang war with their rivals, La Onda. But it was you, wasn't it?"

The killer slowly clapped his hands and chuckled under his breath. As he walked towards Miguel and sat back down, he replied "Bravo, Miguel. She said you were a smart one."

Miguel looked puzzled at the man's words and asked, "Who is *she*?"

The cloaked man stopped clapping and looked away, knowing he had gotten ahead of himself. "That, Miguel, is a subject that we will discuss soon enough. Right now, I feel I need to tell you what I've been busy doing for the last few years. I guess you'd call it a confession. I mean since you have been chasing me for the past 6 years with no leads, you deserve to hear it."

Miguel replied curiously. "One thing I want to know. Why me? Why now? You saved my life when Burk was about to waste me and all you had to do is walk away? Why go to all this trouble just to ease a guilty conscience."

The killer sat silent for a moment. It almost seemed that he was smiling under the veil as he slowly leaned forward and answered, "My grandparents raised me, Miguel. They were good people and they tried to teach me as much as they could about life. My grandfather once told me that a man can lose everything but if he always kept his word, he would always be a man. That's why you are here,

Miguel, and that is why I cannot stop until I have finished the game … no matter how much I want to quit. I don't expect you to understand that right now, but hopefully by the time we're finished, you will."

Chapter 8

The Burning Of An Empire

October 31st, 2007

A steely-eyed man walked up to the gates of Carlos Mentaga's lavish mansion outside of the small West Texas town of Sierra Blanca. His eyes studied the castle-like structure as he reached out and pressed the intercom button.

"I've heard of hiding in plain sight ... but this is ridiculous," he muttered to himself as a Spanish-accented voice came through the gate's intercom speaker.

"Can I help you?"

The visitor turned his attention from the immense building to the security camera. "Senor Mentaga is expecting me. I am the Wolf."

"I see. A moment please, Senor."

The visitor sighed and began to slowly pace back and forth as he waited for the guard to go through the usual security procedures. Finally, the speaker crackled again, "I apologize for the wait, Senor Lobo. Please, come in."

The man stared straight ahead as the massive gates creaked open and the well-paid hit man known only as "The Wolf" stepped inside. His hand brushed against his Beretta 9mm. Its steel slide felt cool against the palm of his hand. It was the only thing in this world that he trusted. They worked as a team and together they had taken more lives than he could remember.

He looked down on the rugged weapon. It had served him well throughout his career as a hit man for the South American drug cartels whose paranoia and mistrust of colleagues had provided him with a steady income. It had also served him before his fall from grace; served him in a time when things were much different than what they were now. A time when he was a soldier … a time when he was the best.

Lieutenant Patrick Tucker was once an asset to the U.S. Armed Forces as a member of an elite SEAL team. Highly decorated during the Vietnam War, the eighteen-year-old had made a mark for himself as an exceptionable asset through his three tour stint. His strict loyalty and ability to follow orders had shown through time and time again as some of his assignments crossed the boundary between acts of war and outright assassination. It was during this time that he was dubbed with his nickname "The Wolf" from his fellow SEALs due to his cunning nature and having survived extremely dangerous solo missions.

Everything he had done had been for his country and he executed his duties with extreme prejudice. His last mission, however, had gone terribly wrong. Although he had survived, the guilt he would carry from that failure would relentlessly haunt him. Lieutenant Patrick Tucker's life would be changed forever.

July 5th, 1989

Tucker and his team plummeted from their high altitude drop into a war-ravaged city in the African country of Liberia. Their orders were simple. Locate and eliminate Rebel General Ruhimbi Turu, a sadistic militant and indiscriminate killer, slashing his way into power.

The hot night air rushed over his face as the SEAL team jumped from the C-130 cargo plane. Lieutenant Tucker began to smell smoke from burning fires that dotted the terrain beneath him. He had been through some of the worst hellholes the world had to offer and, against incredible odds, faced off against some of the maddest men the world had ever seen, but nothing would prepare the Wolf for the chaotic whirlwind of death that raged below them.

The team landed some 2 miles from the war-torn city where General Turu was reported to have taken as his command center. The team moved silently through the grassy fields and into the shadows of the burning village.

As they made their way down a back alley to the commander's hideout, something was happening in the town square that caught Tucker's eye. A group of Turu's soldiers were drinking, laughing loudly as they pulled local children, one by one, out of a large steel cage and tied them to the hood of a burned out truck.

Tucker stopped his team and froze in horror as he watched a drunken soldier chop off the screaming boy's arms and legs. The wailing child was then picked up and thrown into a heap of other children that lay dismembered and dying.

Whether it was witnessing this or the compounded memories of atrocities brought to a head by this inhuman act … whatever the reason, Tucker snapped. A rush of hatred he had never felt before consumed him. His lips curled exposing his clenched teeth. His silver eyes glaring with rage, he raised the barrel of his M-60 A-1 and opened fire on the soldiers, mowing them down.

The shots alerted Turu's troops who began to pour out into the streets like ants, exchanging gunfire with the SEAL team. The firefight lasted for two bloody hours as Wolf and his men stood their ground. The battle was an honorable one, but even the SEALs' extensive training and superior weaponry were no match for the much larger force, leaving only Lieutenant Tucker alive, hiding among the ruins of the battered city with the thoughts of his dead team members lying on the burning streets.

It was his fault they were dead. They had every right to abandon him for giving away their position by firing on the cruel rebel soldiers, but they had stayed. Maybe they understood the reason he decided to fight, but that did not change the fact that they were gone and he could never return home with the guilt of their deaths on his conscience. How could he explain their deaths to the families of the men that trusted him with their lives? How could he justify that they died because of him? He couldn't.

Tucker lay motionless among the dead for two days, waiting for the enemy soldiers to discontinue their search for him. He watched helplessly as his team were dismembered and burned while Turu's soldiers howled and fired their weapons in celebration.

Suddenly, his eyes fixed on a large man in a highly decorated military uniform walking among the saluting soldiers. It was Turu, looking like a peacock as he strutted over to the remains of the mutilated American soldiers and spat on their bodies.

Tucker narrowed his eyes in anger. How dare he desecrate them like that! They were soldiers! His soldiers! He would make them pay! All of them!

That night, the Wolf crept from his hidden position. He was no longer a soldier, but a vicious animal bent on avenging his team's deaths. Shadow-like, he silently worked his way through the burning streets. One at a time, Turu's soldiers fell prey to the razor-edged blade of his Ka-Bar knife. It was almost as if he were a ghost as he made his way to an old motel that was Turu's makeshift command post.

Hunched forward and covered in blood, the Wolf made short work of the General's posted guards. As he entered Turu's bedchambers, his eyes gleamed with an unquenchable blood lust. He stared at the overfed, sleeping form of the murderous general and pulled up the blood-soaked blade of the Ka-Bar. "Good evening, General," he said in a crazed tone, startling the fat man from his sleep.

The bewildered Turu reached for his pistol only to feel a horrendous pain in his upper arm as the Wolf sliced through his shoulder, severing the connective tissue down to the bone. The rebel leader emitted a blood-curdling scream as his now limp arm flopped uselessly by his side.

The Wolf chuckled insanely as he hauled the obese man out of his bed and tied him to a chair in the corner of the room.

"Help me! Please! Someone help me!" Turu cried into the night air, his eyes wild with fear of the vicious beast that had lashed him down.

"Scream all you want, Turu!" the Wolf said as he flicked on the light switch, revealing his blood-drenched form. "Maybe God will save you because no one here will!" The vengeful Wolf relished every moment of the hours ticking away the life of the screaming general as he dismembered him piece by piece.

The morning sun rose on the ravaged town, exposing the horror left by the merciless soldier from the night before. The madman general's troops lay strewn about the streets, their slit throats and punctured bodies chilling Turu's second regiment of troops as they entered the silent village.

Mission accomplished … but at the expense of the deaths of his SEAL team.

By morning the Wolf was well away from the city and heading towards the coast. He knew he would be hunted. He had to get out of Africa as soon as possible. A few days and a merchant ship later, the lone soldier landed on the coast of Vera Cruz, Mexico.

In the years to come he would become a subcontractor for the Columbian drug cartels where his job would be handling "special" situations for the illegal empires.

October 31st, 2007

Three days prior, the Wolf had received word from Javier Melente, the head of the largest Columbian drug cartel, about an ongoing problem with one of their gang affiliates. The "13", as they called themselves, had suffered an unexplained loss of personnel and money over the past few years.

At first, it appeared that a rival gang was trying to take over territory, as usually happens with the mad dog mentality of these street-educated groups, but a survivor of one of these violent episodes had described something totally different. A lone man, clad in eerie attire, was the cause of their troubles. Superstitious stories from the ranks of the now fearful Mexican gang included visions of a white owl before the "ghost" would appear.

The leader of the gang, Carlos Mentaga, had made the call. The Wolf hated him. He had heard of Carlos's brutal methods of transporting cocaine and the exploitation of everyone in the areas he controlled. Nevertheless, he was asked to come and he had a reputation to uphold.

Melente had insisted that he "solve" the problem, no matter what the cost. This caught the interest of the aging hit man. The Wolf was always paid well, but maybe he could make enough with this contract to retire. This would be it. This would be his last job. He had spent the majority of his life in the company of death and it was time to piece together what little bit of life he had left. It was time to quit.

As he walked through the lush gardens of the mansion, the Wolf looked around at Carlos Mentaga's henchmen. He chortled as he walked up the steps and approached the smiling gang leader.

Carlos held out his hand and greeted him, "Hello, Senor Lobo. I trust your trip was pleasant. Please, come in.... make yourself comfortable." The two men walked through the lavish home and into the den where Carlos took a seat across from the quiet hit man. "As you probably already know, I have been having a few problems moving my product."

The Wolf rolled his eyes and sighed, leaning forward to reply, "Don't candy-coat this, Carlos. Your jolly little pirate gang is basically out of business. From what I hear, you lost your last processing lab distributor just days ago and your main distributor is missing. What do you say we cut through the bullshit and get down to business? Pablo told me that you had something to show me … some sort of video with footage of this "ghost"?"

Carlos was infuriated at the condescending words of the Wolf. How dare he talk to him so bluntly in his own house and in front of his men, but he held his tongue. This was his last resort to holding on to his crumbling drug empire. Besides, the Wolf was not a man to cross. He remembered the stories of dozens of armed men killed by the Wolf and even some employers who thought him to be less than his reputation.

Carlos stood and walked over to his big screen television. He pressed the power button and turned to the Wolf. "This was sent to me this morning. Maybe it will help you locate him."

As the DVD played, the Wolf sat quietly as he intently watched the images of a large, wide-shouldered man, his hands clasped behind his back, standing in an old cemetery. He studied the man … a gray Fedora hat hung just above his cat-like eyes and over his face he wore a surgeon's mask that covered his nose and lower half of his face. Clad around his body was a gray trench coat, flapping gently in a breeze that whistled over the marble monuments and tombstones that sprinkled the ground behind him.

"Spooky guy!" the Wolf chuckled as the veiled man in the recording began to speak.

"Good evening, Carlos. I'm sure you realize by now that the reason your empire is crumbling is more than just a rival gang take-over or some bullshit stories passed around by your people. For now, I don't really think it's necessary for me to give you a reason why I hate you. Rest assured, when we finally meet in person, I'll be more than happy to tell you before you draw your last breath … that's if your employers don't kill you first. I'm sure they're not too happy with you right now."

"Oh, I almost forgot I am sending you a present!" the man in the video continued. "It's sort of a Happy Halloween gift. I'm sure you'll love it! Anyway, enjoy what few days you have left, Carlos. I'll be seeing you soon."

Carlos stopped the DVD and began to pace back and forth, waiting for a response from the Wolf. The silent man sat pondering what he had just seen. It was true … the stories from the superstitious gang members were not imagined at all. He would really have his work cut out for him on this one. This "ghost", this madman, was driven by something Carlos had done and, knowing Carlos, there was probably a good reason for the cloaked man's hatred for him.

He looked up at the pacing gang leader and spoke. "Seven million. All in advance." The Wolf knew Carlos' back was against the wall and he was out of options. The chaos this "ghost" had created in his organization was closing in on him and it showed.

Carlos's eyes widen at the amount. "*Seven million!* How about the fillings out of my fucking teeth, Cavron!"

The Wolf smiled and stood up from the couch. "This ghost of yours has cost you a lot of money already. Under the circumstances, Carlos, I think it's a bargain, considering what the Cartel will do to you if you keep losing money … or what this guy will do to you if he finds you. It's clear that he already knows where you live. Or, if you want, I can go back and tell the Cartel you have this matter under control. It's your call."

Weighing his choices, Carlos paced wildly in a circle, rubbing his neck with shaking hands. Making the only decision he could, he looked at his personal bodyguard, Enyo, and pointed toward the back of the house. "Get the money, Enyo."

Enyo tried to argue but was cut short as Mentaga screamed something in Spanish that the Wolf did not understand to his confidant. Enyo clinched his teeth and reluctantly obeyed the order, exiting to retrieve the money.

Carlos moved to a mini-bar in the far corner of the living room and poured himself a drink. The Wolf had a private laugh at Carlos' plight as he watched the drug dealer wipe his sweaty forehead. Carlos uttered a deep sigh and turned to continue his conversation with his hit man. "How long will it take you to find this bastard, Senor Lobo?"

"No more than a week. I will find him. Any special instructions?"

Carlos set his drink down and curled his lips back. "I want you to cut his head off and bring it to me. As a matter of fact, I want you to cut him into pieces! Can you do that?"

The hit man slowly nodded, "I think I can handle that."

Enyo returned with two large briefcases and sat them down in front of the hit man. The Wolf turned and pointed to the television. "I'd like that DVD, if you don't mind. I believe I can find the location of that graveyard."

Carlos retrieved the disc and handed it to the Wolf who shoved it into his inside jacket pocket.

"Nice doing business with you, Carlos," he chuckled as he picked up the two cash-filled briefcases and walked towards the door.

"Don't you want to count it?" Carlos questioned.

The Wolf turned and gave Carlos a look that chilled him to the bone. "I know you don't like me, Carlos. Trust me, the feeling is mutual. But if you try to screw me on this, I will deliver you to this "ghost" myself."

Carlos and Enyo watched the laughing man walk out of the mansion and toward the main gate. Once he was out of sight, Carlos released his anger by shoving the gigantic TV, screen down, to the floor with a crashing sound. "That arrogant bastard! He had better do his fucking job!"

Enyo watched his employer start to smash anything breakable in the room. He tried to quiet his frustrated boss and friend by saying, "Don't worry, Senor Carlos. I have already started two new processing labs. And they did not find King's body at his mansion so that means he is probably hiding out. As soon as he shows up, we can open up shop again. Then we can replace the Cartel's money."

Carlos held his hand to his forehead and sighed as he spoke to Enyo. "You do not understand, to the Cartel it is more than money. It is the ability to control your territory. If the Lobo does not kill this fucking curse, we are dead men!"

A voice from one of Carlos' men interrupted their conversation. "Senor Carlos, this package came for you a few minutes ago." Carlos looked at the box and motioned for the guard to set it on the table.

Enyo walked over and opened the thick cardboard container. He looked inside and spoke in a shaky voice to his boss, "Senor Menatga, you had better come have a look at this." Carlos sighed and walked over to his bodyguard whose face had paled as he fixed on the box's contents.

"Look at what?" Carlos shouted as he walked over and peered inside. His eyes narrowed in disgust as the dismembered head of Darrel King silently stared back at him; his mouth open in an eternal scream. Carlos closed his eyes and steadied himself on the counter top, leaning his head back.

"What have I done to deserve this? What? I am a businessman! This fucking "ghost"! What have I done to this crazy bastard?"

Chapter 9

The King is Dead

October 29th, 2007

Darrel King, or "The King" as he called himself, arrived at his home on the outskirts of Wharton, Texas. His diamond-grill smile shone brightly as he stepped out of his limo and adjusted his coat in front of his splendid, two-story mansion. Tonight was a good night. He was throwing the first in a series of parties for the approach of Halloween.

Darrel, once a street hood from the projects in Houston, was now enjoying a life of excess as the new cocaine distributor and processor for the "13" gang in Texas. He had been warned when he took the job about the "ghost" that had all but wiped out his predecessors, but he had only laughed and shrugged it off, calling the stories "VooDoo Bullshit."

Darrel had assured his new employer, Carlos Menatga, that he could handle the job, that it would take more than a white boy with a few guns to bring him down. The possible threat of danger didn't bother King, who only cared about one thing—money ... and lots of it. His knowledge of the drug trade was vast and he turned a healthy profit from his efficient army of street dealers. He was also valuable at processing the 13's pure product in a hidden underground lab that worked day and night behind his home on the vast stretches of his property, out of view of the authorities.

Although King had few social skills, he loved to throw parties. This one in particular was huge. 153 guests were enjoying themselves inside as King stepped onto the second story balcony, holding his arms toward the ceiling as the crowd cheered him on.

"Yeeah, yeeah! Da king's in da house, Niggas!" he screeched. The party guests greeted him with loud applause, chanting his name as he made his way to the lower floor to mingle with his guests.

Outside, the fog had set in on the cold October night, shadowing the silent advance of a man cloaked in gray trench coat as he neared the noisy house. The killer stopped and crouched, scanning the front of the house, undetected by the three guards and limo driver that were busy making small talk.

He knew that the wild party inside would mask any noise he made, but the coke lab behind the house would be another story. He sat motionless for a moment, waiting for the best moment to launch his assault. For the last two days he had been carefully planning his attack sequence in an abandoned work shed some three miles away.

The fog could not have moved in at a better time as he pulled out his silenced .45, closing his eyes and clearing his mind for a moment. Then, with a whip of his trench coat, he slipped across the sod field towards the limo, staying low so that the large car would provide him cover.

Suddenly, he stood erect and touched the trigger. A red beam of light shot from the laser sight on the silenced pistol, painting the target mark on the first guard's forehead. The pistol chattered as the sizzling bullets found their victims, spraying geysers of blood as they passed through the bodies of the three guards who had no time to react to the lightning-fast attack.

The fat limo driver was frozen with fear as his friends fell into slumping piles in front of his eyes. His jaw dropped, trying to scream as he turned directly into the beam of the red laser. A click of the gun's action sent three slugs into the fat man's lungs, rendering him unable to speak. The limo driver staggered, collapsing to the ground, as the killer rounded the long-black car and began searching the dying man's pockets for the limo keys. A jingle made him smile underneath his veil as he found the keys and rose to his feet.

The limo driver gasped as he tried to curse the man with his emptied lungs. The killer raised his pistol and growled, "Sorry, dude … wrong place, wrong time … wrong friends." He squeezed the trigger, splattering the back of the fat man's skull onto the ground.

The cloaked man quickly surveyed the grounds for more guards. To his surprise, there were none. He looked down at the three guards who lay twisted on the ground and his eyes moved to their weapons. "UZI!" he said to himself as he grabbed the sub-machine pistol and extra magazines from one of the dead guards.

Getting into the limo to execute the second part of his plan, he cranked it and drove around to the back of the house where a large, steel door leading to a fake storm cellar covered the hidden coke lab.

He carefully rolled the car's front wheels onto the slanted door, stopping any chance of escape by the occupants inside. He killed the engine of the heavy automobile and stepped out into the cold night.

He could barely believe the lack of security around the house. But then, it was not too surprising. This area was remote and desolate, with nothing but flat ground as far as the eye could see. He had also heard that King was arrogant and thought that no one would have the balls to threaten him. He thought wrong.

After greeting his guests, King had gone up to his second story private party room. He dipped his head and danced as the loud music thumped in his ears as he crossed the floor. Taking a seat on a ornate throne he had purchased at an antique auction some time back, King picked up a mirror that had a massive amount of powdered cocaine on it's reflective surface and snorted a line.

He looked to his left at a smiling young girl. His mouth widened into a grin as he beckoned her over to him. "Hey baby! What's your name?" he yelled in her ear over the noise of the music.

She smiled and answered, "Laura! Are you the King?"

He slapped his hands together and laughed, exposing his sparkling grill work. "You know it, baby! Hey, let's go back to a more private room! What do you say?"

The girl nodded in agreement as King exited his throne and led her out of the noisy party room and into his master bedroom.

Now that the drug lab was secured, the cloaked man was at the front door of the mansion. He slowly reached for the doorknob. Turning it, the door opened with a click. A loud burst of rap music assaulted his senses from inside of the house.

He sat the UZI down on the step and slid a large, heavy bag from over his shoulder. The bag, weighing 25 pounds, was a mixture of 10 pounds of high explosives smothered in a tightly wrapped shell of razor-sharp fletchettes. He pressed a button on the top of the bag. The LED armed and ready indicator responded with a green glow and the deadly apparatus sounded a quick, high-pitched beep. Then, in one quick move, he opened the door and hurled the massive explosive device inside.

The oblivious partygoers never saw the object as it soared over their heads and exploded in mid-air, raining down a hail of deadly shrapnel and the steel darts ripping through them.

The killer grabbed up the UZI, pulled the .45 from under his coat, and burst into the house. His eyes moved from target to target as he extinguished the lives of anyone that remained alive.

His attention suddenly was drawn to the upper floor, where he saw four men racing across the balcony behind the upstairs railing. As they opened fire on the killer, he ducked behind the staircase avoiding the rounds that spattered around him. The cloaked man knew he had to act before the men could make it down the stairs.

He took a deep breath and bolted from his hiding place, raising the UZI and emptying the magazine into the fast-approaching men. The attackers fell screaming as the 9 mm rounds perforated their bodies.

A shout from across the room then drew his attention as King's brother appeared in the kitchen door and opened fire with his TEC-9, spraying rounds in all directions. The loosed projectiles from the carbine struck the cloaked man's chest, sending him stumbling backwards over a dead partygoer and to the floor.

Trip, as they called him, thought he had slain the aggressor but, unfortunately for him, the man's coat had a surprise underneath. A thick layer of Kevlar coated the inside of the gray jacket.

Trip started to run off at the mouth, shouting taunts and curses at the man as he walked across the party floor, reloading his weapon. "Thought you was bad, huh, mutha fucka? Got yo ass shot what you did!"

Reaching the fallen killer, his taunts were silenced by fear as the barrel of the Franchi SPAS-15 appeared from under the man's gray trench coat. Trip raised his weapon to fire but it was too late as the volley of armor-piercing slugs cut him almost in half, the force of the impact knocking him across the room. Bruised, but otherwise unharmed, the veiled man stumbled to his feet and reloaded the shotgun with another drum mag.

The rumbling sound of frantic steps came from the top of the stairs as the startled, second floor partiers tried to escape the mayhem. Moving quickly to the foot of the staircase to meet the hysterical crowd, the gunman opened fire on the screaming guests, cutting them down as the massive shotgun unleashed its hellish contents on them.

He then wasted no time making his way to the second floor. Topping the stairs, a shot came from his right, striking him in his exposed leg. He spun from the impact, landing on his back as the well-positioned guard emptied the magazine of his MP-5 into the intruder's bulletproof coat.

The killer rolled and quickly fired three rounds from the massive shotgun. The guard's head exploded from the impact of the rounds. His lifeless body stood for a moment, then, with a quivering step, fell over the handrail to join the rest of the dead on the first floor with a thud.

The cloaked man slapped in another magazine of the deadly fletchette rounds. He looked down at his own wound; it had passed through his calf, but was bleeding badly.

"At least I don't have to dig this one out!" he muttered to himself as he pulled the veil from around his face and tightly wrapped the bleeding leg.

With clenched teeth, the killer got to his feet, trying to shake off the pain from the wound. He pulled up the shotgun and crept slowly towards the entrance to the upstairs party room.

Oblivious in his bedroom, King had felt the rumble from the earlier explosion and the disturbance had brought an abrupt halt to his sexual interlude with the young blonde. He now crouched behind his throne with uneasy breath. His shaking hands wrapped around the grip of his chromed Beretta 9mm pistol.

He had raised the weapon toward the door when he was startled by the young woman's touch on his shoulder. His finger squeezed in reflex, firing the weapon. "Fuck!" he shouted as he frantically darted the shaking pistol towards the door as a voice just outside the room spoke to him.

"Hey there, King! Are you feeling the love in there?"

King sneered and shouted back, "Come on in here, mutha fucka! Get you some of dis!" The angered King fired at the door in desperation, only to be answered by a laugh from the killer outside.

"Hey, uh, King? Maybe you shouldn't waste all of your ammo on the wall?"

King looked at the young girl and reached into his sock, pulling out a snub-nosed .25 pistol. He gave it to her and pointed to a couch adjacent to the door. "Ok, girl, this is what I want you to do. Get behind that couch over there. When he comes in, shoot him in the fucking back. Got it?" he whispered.

The girl nodded, slipped across the dark room and hid behind the couch.

The cloaked man knew that King wouldn't come out from his position of safety, so he had only one choice. Rush him. He pulled up the SPAS-15 and checked it. He only had one magazine left, but that was enough.

He steadied himself and took a deep breath. Then, in one quick move, he broke into the room, firing rounds towards the back wall. The bullets whizzed around King's head like a swarm of angry bees.

Suddenly, a thud hit him from behind, causing him to drop the shotgun. He wheeled around to see the skinny, blonde woman holding a smoking .25 pistol.

"Bitch!" he yelled as he grabbed her hand with his iron grip and twisted it backwards, breaking it in a crackle of bones. With his free hand he snatched the shotgun up and raised it towards King's hiding place.

King heard the woman cry out and stood up from his hidden position behind the chair, only to come face to face with the barrel of the massive shotgun. He screamed as the barrel exploded in a flash of orange flame. The slugs tore his legs in half at the knee, sending the pain-stricken man howling to the ground.

The cloaked man dropped the shotgun and wheeled back around to the sobbing woman. He pulled out his Ka-Bar Warthog knife and slammed the wide blade into her neck. Her cries turned to a gurgle as the blade severed her arteries and filled her windpipe with a wave of blood. He withdrew the blade and quickly sheathed it.

As the woman began to weave, the killer grabbed her by her bleeding neck and shoved her through the sheetrock wall with a powerful thrust. He watched as her body twitched, hanging out of the hole in the wall like a mounted animal trophy.

The sound of sputtered coughing came from the back of the room where King struggled to breath as he bled out. His eyes fixed on the cloaked figure that stepped around the huge chair and knelt down over him.

"Damn, King. That has got to hurt!"

King sneered and spit a mouthful of blood into the man's face. "Fuck you, Bitch!" he weakly muttered and grinned, exposing the now bloodstained diamonds embedded in his teeth. The killer wiped the blood from his face and looked into the eyes of the arrogant drug dealer.

"You know what your problem is, King? It's your mouth!" He clamped his hand over King's mouth and pulled out the black-bladed knife from its sheath. "Maybe you would be better off without it!"

A muffled scream emitted from under the gloved hand as the killer drew back the Ka-Bar and plunged it into King's throat. The cloaked man gave the wide blade a violent twist, opening up the arteries in King's neck.

"Not such a smart ass now are you, King?" The cloaked man said as he withdrew the knife and blood poured from the gaping wound. "I have a job for you, King. You're going to help me send a message," he informed the dying man as he proceeded to completely cut off King's head with the surgically-sharp Ka-Bar.

The killer reached down, picked the severed head up by the ears and looked into its twitching eyes as the last glimmer of life ebbed away. He then deposited the detached member into a thick plastic bag pulled from his trench coat.

He took his time as he picked up his shotgun and painfully limped out of the room. He reached the top of the stairs and stopped for a moment to gaze at the silent mob that lay dead below him.

"They probably had nothing to do with this asshole ... just here for the party," he muttered to himself as he made his way down the stairs. He reached the door and turned back once more. For a moment, he felt sorry for them. A few years ago he was one of these people. Like them, he had tried to sort out the problems in his life with alcohol and illegal chemicals. Like them, he was dead, but dead on the inside.

He shook himself out of his trance and hobbled outside. His job was not over. The drug lab was next. He would enjoy this. This marked the end of the 13's foothold in Texas. Even though they had expanded far into other states, this would be an accomplishment far greater than anything the police could have done. Like the rogue pawn on the chessboard, he did not have to follow the same rules law enforcement must obey.

His methods may be crude and outside of the law, but they were effective ... very effective.

In the drug lab one of the chemists screamed to a guard as they frantically pushed and beat on the jammed lab entrance. "Why won't the damn door open?"

Suddenly, a horrifying sound came from the back of the underground facility. The twelve occupants' faces contorted with fear as they watched a huge vapor cloud pour over the lab floor.

Another of the drug-making workers cried out as he quickly shut off the all burners in the room, "What the hell? Someone is pouring methylene in the ventilation system!"

The chemists and guards began to scream for help as they beat on the blocked steel door. One of the guards looked back as the last of 40 gallons of highly flammable liquid splashed from the vent pipe in the roof. He spied an object the size of a coke can, dangling by a string. Its blinking green light sent a chill up his spine as he ran through the room and jumped, trying to grab it.

"It's a bomb! It's a bomb!"

A voice from the other side of the steel door silenced the occupants as they backed away to listen.

"You guys could have been anything you wanted to! Probably helped cure some horrible disease in a legit lab somewhere or become respected physicians. But no, you had to go to work for a dope-dealing piece of shit! What a waste. Now your fate will be the same as his. Enjoy Hell! I heard it's warm this time of year."

The killer limped away from the blocked lab entrance and pulled out a small box from an upper pocket of his trench coat. Holding it up, he flipped back the safety cover and pressed the red button underneath. A muffled blast came from the lab followed by a bright, orange glow that exploded into a huge fireball, lighting up the night sky.

The veiled man then retrieved the two remaining 20 gallon drums of the methylene he had stashed earlier and made his way to the front door of the huge estate. He paused for a moment and then doused what was left of the mansion's entryway with the flammable liquid.

He retreated into the yard and pulled out his cigarette lighter. With a single flick that both opened the lighter's lid and stuck the flint, he tossed it onto the methylene-soaked floor, igniting it in a rush of hot wind.

"The King *is* dead," the killer muttered as he reached down and picked up the bag that held the late coke dealer's head.

Chapter 10

The Snare

November 3rd, 2007

Agent Miguel Perez and his partner, Larry Jones, sat at the desks in their small FBI office in Dallas, Texas. Perez, the younger of the two men, got up from his computer and walked over to the back wall of the office where crime scene photos of a case they had been chained to for six years were plastered.

Miguel's eyes searched the photos as he had done a thousand times, looking for any clue, any bit of evidence, anything at all that he might have missed. As he looked at the images of victims' bodies in the various motel rooms, a feeling of frustration crept over him. They hadn't gotten any closer to apprehending the perp, much less naming a suspect. They only knew the "how" of these crimes; the who and why were as much a mystery as ever.

He let out a sigh and scratched his head as he walked to the office door, looking out over the other agents working at their desks. The confidence he had when he was assigned to this case so many years ago had turned to frustration.

He looked back at his partner and lamented, "We're never going to catch this guy, Larry. Six hundred murders in seven years … and we have nothing."

Larry stopped typing and swiveled around in his chair, his eyes following Miguel as he moved back to the photo-covered wall.

"What do you mean nothing?" Larry replied. "We have a mountain of evidence."

Miguel shook his head and returned to his seat. "One guy in Humble who described him as wearing a gray hat and trench coat. We know he apparently uses a silenced .45, although we can't be sure since he always recovers his slugs. We think he lures alleged molesters to a motel room using one of a thousand online chatrooms … almost impossible to trace since he uses the motel's Internet services."

Miguel continued, "Oh, here is our one big piece of evidence. He only strikes during the winter months. To sum it up, we know nothing about the perp … nothing! This guy might as well be a ghost."

Larry rubbed his chin and replied, "He wants to kill … we know *that*. Sooner or later he'll get enough … they all do. It won't be long until he wants some kind of publicity or something. He'll screw up sooner or later, then he's ours."

Miguel shook his head and leaned back, rubbing his face with his hands. "I don't know, Larry? Maybe we should leave him alone. Almost every one of his victims has had some kind of past linked to sex crimes. I mean, we're speculating that this guy traps them by pretending to be an underage girl or boy. His victims were up to no good when they walked in, right?"

Larry narrowed his eyes and leaned forward, rubbing his hands together. "It's *still* murder, Miguel! No matter how you slice it, people like this rarely ever stick to one track. It's only a matter of time until he gets bored and changes his MO. Today, it's child predators; tomorrow, it's cab drivers. You know what I mean?"

Miguel stopped rubbing his face and opened his eyes, seeing a stern look on Larry's face. He cracked a smile and waved his hand at Larry. "I'm not saying what he is doing is right by any means. I'm just tired. Just thinking out loud."

Larry nodded in agreement and turned to look at the wall as he spoke to Miguel. "Same here, man. It's been a long six years. You're right about one thing … something good thing has come out of this case. Have you ever watched that "Dateline" tv special about catching online child predators? It's been on several times in the last several months.

Miguel replied, "Yeah, I've seen it. Pretty crazy, isn't it?"

Larry chuckled as he turned back to his computer. "Yeah, it is. The funny part is how it all came about. A couple of years ago, some television executive found out about our boy and thought it would be a good idea to get with a few of his police connections and, wham, he has a hit. What do you think about that?"

Miguel chuckled, turning back to the report he had been working on. "We should have copyrighted it."

The two men were laughing at the joke when Miguel's phone rang. He held up his finger to shush his laughing partner and answered the phone in a light-hearted tone. "Agent Miguel Perez. Can I help you?"

Miguel's face had a puzzled look as the voice on the other end spoke softly. "Hello, Miguel … it's been a long time, hasn't it? I would say about 7 years."

Miguel's mood suddenly changed. Something about the voice caused a lump to form in his throat. He looked at Larry with a curious look and answered, "Who is this?"

The voice paused for a moment, then continued, "Well ... the papers call me "The Texas Motel Killer". If you need a name, then I guess that will do for now."

Miguel leaned back in his seat and smiled. A lot of people had called him, claiming to be the killer. Most were crazies whose lives were so mundane they would gladly take the risk of imprisonment for a few moments in the spotlight.

"Ok, Sir, if you are who you claim to be, tell me something about the murders."

The voice on the other end chuckled and replied, "The men were all killed with a .45 automatic and they were all potential child molesters. I prefer to call them roaches."

Miguel motioned to Larry to start the routine trace and continued, "Sir, anyone who has read the paper or watched television in the past six years would know that."

The voice sat silent for a moment, then answered, "Did the papers mention that the victims all had the letters "M" and "I" cut into their feet?"

The hair on Miguel's neck stood up as he realized that this *was* the killer on the other end of the line. He waved frantically at Larry and put the conversation on speakerphone.

"Uh, ok ... you have my attention. What can I do for you?"

The voice chuckled again at Miguel's stammering voice. "Easy, Miguel! I know you're tracing this call and I'll stay on long enough for you to get a fix on me. That translates into about three minutes if I'm right, so I'll keep this brief. I want to have a meeting ... tomorrow ... just you and me. Does that interest you?"

Miguel watched Larry's computer as it locked on to the phone number, revealing an address.

"Yes, it would. Where do you want to meet?"

The voice answered, "I'll let you know ... that's enough for now."

The call ended with a click as Larry clapped his hands together. "Got it! 4434 Harry Hines Boulevard ... Room 202 ... the Baker Motel."

The two agents wasted no time as they grabbed their coats and ran out of the office.

Miguel's Dodge Charger came to a screeching halt in the parking lot of the old Baker Motel, a known haven for drug dealing and prostitution. The two agents pulled their weapons and made their way up the stairs to the numbered "202".

Larry stood in front with his weapon ready. He nodded and Miguel knocked loudly on the door.

"FBI! Open the door!!"

The two waited for a response, but the room was silent.

Larry stepped back and kicked hard, ripping the door from its hinges. In a quick, well-trained entrance, the two agents rushed into the room pointing their weapons in all directions.

Larry patted Miguel on the shoulder and pointed to the bathroom where a thick cloud of steam was boiling out from under the door. The two agents cautiously approached the door and gently swung it open. Their eyes came to rest on a dead man lying in the bathtub. His mouth was open in a silent scream as the hot water poured over his head and into the red-stained tub in which he lay.

"Dammit!" Larry shouted as he holstered his pistol and pulled out his cell phone to call for a crime scene investigation unit.

Miguel knelt down to check the victim and slowly shook his head as he gazed at the gaping bullet hole. Over the past six years he had seen this same scenario time and time again, and he already knew what caliber weapon had taken the man's life, a .45 automatic.

Miguel looked around the room. The floor was littered with a variety of fast food containers and clothes. The desk where the computer sat had a small tray beside it with three lines of powder rowed out.

"Must be cocaine," he thought to himself as he examined the creamy color of the substance.

He rubbed the top of his head in thought as his partner closed his cell phone and spoke. "They're sending the evidence team. They should be here in about ten minutes."

Miguel nodded as he noticed something on the bed. He walked over to it and saw that a stack of Polaroid photos lay fanned out like a deck of cards.

"Hey, Larry! Take a look at this!"

The two agents examined the pictures with disgust. They were sex photos of the now dead victim with an array of children.

"I can't say I feel sorry for the bastard," Miguel stated as he walked to the window and looked out over the city. He paused and then said, "He's here, Larry. Somewhere close, watching us."

Larry looked up at his partner from his examination of the blood trail leading to the bathroom. "What makes you so sure?"

Miguel sighed and continued scanning the city street. "Just a feeling I have. He wants to see us in person."

Miguel's cell phone startled him as it rang. He flipped it open and answered, "Agent Perez speaking."

A now familiar voice was on the other end. "Hello Miguel. I think by now you know I am who I say I am. Do you still want to talk?"

Miguel pursed his lips. "Yeah, I do."

The voice replied in a lighter tone, "Good! Tomorrow morning … Jacksonville, Texas … 8 AM. Don't be late. I'll give you, and you alone, instructions from there. By the way, I left you a note there that you might find interesting. Be sure you read it."

The voice said goodbye, ending the call with a click.

"Who was that?" Larry asked as he walked into the trashed-out living room.

"It was him. He wants to meet me in the morning in Jacksonville … and he wants me to come alone."

Larry nodded, "Alright, we'll worry about that later. I need the keys to your car to get your camera out of the trunk."

Miguel handed him the keys and began to look around the room for the note the killer said he had left for him.

Walking across the parking lot to Miguel's Dodge Charger, Larry listened for a moment to the approaching sirens of the crime scene unit. "About damn time," he muttered as he stuck the key in the lock.

He looked down at the door window and spotted a folded piece of yellow paper. He looked around to see if anyone was looking. "Miguel was right, the killer was here," he thought to himself as he reached down and unfolded the note. Larry's eyes grew wide as he read the words.

"Shit!" he muttered and pulled out his cell phone. He paced frantically as he dialed the number and waited for an answer. He was just about to hang up when a scratchy voice on the other end answered, "What's up, boss?"

Larry turned his head towards the motel and spoke. "Hey, Burk, I need you to run a tap on my partner's cell phone … and get the team ready. I'll meet you guys in Tyler, Texas, about 4 am. You think you can handle that?"

Agent Burk sat on the edge of his bed and pushed his long hair out of his eyes. "Yeah, I'll get right on it. Who did you want the tap on?"

Larry answered, "My partner, Miguel Perez."

Burk closed his eyes and grinned at the name. He hated Perez with a passion. "That little punk wetback? No problem. So, what's going on?"

Larry looked at the note and crumbled it in his hand. "We have a problem."

November 4th, 2007–8 AM

Miguel pulled into the small town of Jacksonville, Texas. He was deep in thought about the meeting that was supposed to take place in a few hours. He had discussed with Larry about using a tactical team to raid the suspect's hideout but Larry insisted that he should go alone, with him as backup as soon as he had the location.

This was a strange as Larry was always the first to recommend a large force to surprise a suspect. Larry told him that this might be a trick to see if he was trustworthy enough to come alone and, if a large team approached, it might scare the suspect off and be the last chance they would have to catch him.

As he pulled over and waited for the call that would give him the final instructions of where the meeting would take place, Miguel still thought something was odd about his partner's suggestions and seemingly unusual behavior, but he trusted his judgment. After all, he was far more experienced in these matters.

His phone chiming at his side broke Miguel's train of thought. He looked at his watch at the time. 8 AM. He flipped his phone open and answered. "Agent Perez."

A chuckle came from the other end of the phone line. "Good morning, Miguel. Are you ready for our little chat?"

The agent sternly answered, "Just give me directions and I'll find you."

Miguel pulled out his notepad and carefully wrote down the directions. He closed his pen and dialed Larry's cell phone number but there was no answer. He tried again and again, but still Larry didn't pick up.

"Where the hell are you, man?" he muttered through his clenched teeth and slammed his phone shut, wondering what to do now.

He made his decision. He would go alone. The thought of chasing this man any longer was unimaginable. He pulled out his .45 and chambered a round into the barrel with a metallic clink. "I hope you're there," he muttered as he got back in the Charger and sped off down the highway toward the meeting place.

The killer clicked off his cell phone and laid it on the table where he was sitting. His eyes moved around the old wooden farmhouse that once belonged to the deceased Ybalde Servin.

He reached into his pocket and pulled out a tattered picture. His eyes began to fill with tears as he smiled and gently touched the faces of the woman in the photograph. "I finally found him, Mayella. I kept my promise." He kissed the image and carefully placed the photo back in the inside pocket of his gray trench coat.

An eerie feeling crept over him as if someone was watching him. He jerked his head towards the front door. "Shit!" he shouted, kicking himself backwards from the table as a man holding two silenced 9mm Berettas rushed inside with his pistols chattering.

The bullets thudded into him and found an opening in his Kevlar-lined trench coat. The cloaked man lurched from the shot and pulled his .45, scrambling behind an old, upright gun safe. He whipped the pistol up and touched off three rounds into nothing.

"This guy is good," he thought to himself as he looked down at the slowly spreading red patch on his shirt.

He knew he could not take this man head on. This was a professional … and a very experienced one. If he were to survive, he would have to out-think him.

Suddenly, a loud voice came from the kitchen. "You disappoint me! I thought you would be faster than that!"

His taunting was quickly silenced by a volley of rounds that splattered through the wall, sending a cloud of splinters and paint chips onto the ducking hit man.

"Is that fast enough for you!" the cloaked man shouted.

The unknown assailant smiled at the man's words. "You should feel lucky! With the money I am making from killing you, I can get out of this business for good. Well, it's time to say goodbye!"

He whirled around kitchen door, raining hot lead into the heavy steel box as he ran towards it. He slammed into the side of the gun safe and slowly peered around it, hoping to come face to face with his target. To his surprise, there was nothing there except the wooden floor … and a pool of blood.

He traced the drops as they dotted their way across the floor and up the stairs. "Got you now," he whispered as he slowly made his way up to the second floor.

The cloaked man had fled to an upstairs room, locking the door behind him. He looked around the room … he needed some diversion to occupy his attacker's attention for only a fraction of a second.

He pulled his .45 into view and studied it. If the hit man had on body armor this weapon would be useless. Then, he remembered that he had stashed his SPAS-15, loaded with sharpened steel fletchettes, in the room for just such an emergency.

His eyes came to rest on a bright sunbeam that shone through the window of the dusty room. Suddenly, an idea hit him. "Yes! That'll work!" he thought to himself as he pulled off his trench coat and hat.

The hit man crept silently through the hallway, his pistols steady as he approached the door of the room his target was in. He knelt down to look through the keyhole but it was blocked with paper. "Impressive," he thought to himself as he rose to his feet.

He took a step back, causing an old floor board to creak under him. He froze in his tracks as he listened intently for any movement on the other side of the door. He waited a few seconds. Then he heard it, a scuffle that came from the left side of the room. He raised his pistols and readied himself. With a powerful kick, he swung the door open, rushed into the room and instantly opened fire on the trench coat and hat that stood silhouetted by the wide beam of morning sunlight.

A sick feeling hit him as he realized he had made a fatal mistake.

From his left, the thundering barrel of the SPAS-15 roared as it sent a swarm of steel darts into his hands, disintegrating them in a spray of blood.

The hit man sent by the "13" gang drug dealers looked at the mangled flesh and blood where his hands once were and chuckled. For the first time in his life, the Wolf had been outsmarted. It was over. He turned to face the killer who now chambered another round. He smiled as he raised his arms out from his sides and uttered two words. "Finish it!"

The shotgun thundered over and over, sending the deadly fletchettes piercing his body, slicing through his organs, and hurling his lifeless body crashing out of the nearby window.

The killer lowered the smoking shotgun and fell to his knees. "Who the hell was that?" he spoke aloud as he reached down to the aching bullet wound in his side. He pulled himself to his feet and slowly walked over to the window, grabbing his coat and hat.

"What the Hell!" he muttered as his eyes focused on a group of armed men approaching the house. "That lying bastard Miguel!" he whispered as he quickly put on the coat and hat and ran into the hall as a hailstorm of bullets and suppression grenades poured into the house.

Chapter 11

The Bond of a Promise

Miguel sat silent. His head felt like it was about to explode. Everything he had done for the past six years had been almost for nothing. His partner, who he looked up to as a father figure and mentor, turned out to be nothing more than a drug-dealing murderer who had basically ordered his death.

Then there was this man in front of him. Six years ago, when he started this investigation, Miguel thought he was the sum of all evil, a deadly spider that trapped and took away life, only to find out that the man had been waging some kind of personal war from his past. A war that destroyed everything and everyone that had gotten in his way and, from what he could gather, the war was far from over.

To a point, he understood him. He seemed to have been a good man once, but good men do bad things when their worlds are stripped away from them.

Miguel raised his head and spoke in a soft voice, "How much blood is enough?"

The cloaked man leaned back in his seat at the question and sighed, "It will never be enough, Miguel. No measure of blood will ever stop the pain I carry around with me. My only hope is that maybe, just maybe, when I die God will forgive me. Until then, I have no reason to stop. Everything that was good in me died along with my Mayella and Isabel … and it's not coming back.

Miguel realized he had heard those names before. "What was your wife's name again?"

The killer leaned forward and stared hard into Miguel's eyes as if to drill the name into him. "Her name was Mayella Vargas Perez. Her mother's name was Adrianna Perez and her father's name was Ricardo Lingua Perez. Why do you want to know? Do you recognize her name?"

Miguel was stunned at hearing these names. This could not be. Miguel knew the names and knew them well. These were his family's names! How did this man know his family? No one could. The Catholic orphanage he had grown up in had sealed his records. He had only found out about his past himself from a kind nun who allowed him to see his orphanage file.

Then it hit him. He looked at the photo on his lap of the scarred woman, then back to the now softened face of the killer. Miguel's eyes filled with tears as he realized who the woman was and why the man had gone to so much trouble to find him.

"She was my sister, wasn't she?"

The killer nodded slowly at the question and reached out gently, placing his hand on Miguel's shoulder. "When we were together she used to cry in her sleep. She always mentioned one name ... Miguel. I asked her who Miguel was and she told me the story. She never stopped thinking about you."

The cloaked man took his hand from Miguel's shoulder and reached into his coat pocket producing another photo. "I never knew why I kept this, but I'm glad I did. Here ... this belongs to you."

Miguel took the photo and studied it. His lips quivered as he looked at the old photo. His mother stood in the image with her beautiful smile and long black hair. He could still hear her voice as she sang him to sleep every night. His sister had her arms lovingly wrapped around the young boy in front of her.

He could not hold his emotions back any longer. The tears began to pour from his eyes and his hands started to shake as a wave of grief rolled over him. He covered his face and sobbed, "Why are you telling me this? Why? I had tried to put my past behind me! Oh, God! Why are you doing this to me?"

The cloaked man hung his head for a moment, then answered, "I made a promise a long time ago to my wife that I would find you. It took me seven long years to do it, but I found you. That's why you are here, Miguel."

The grief-stricken agent raised his red, tear-filled eyes and watched as the cloaked man stood up and walked slowly to a sheet-covered object on the far wall.

"So what happens now?" Miguel asked.

The man pulled the sheet free from the object. It was an old crematorium furnace. Two steel boxes were welded on the top of the furnace with a crank handle between them.

The cloaked man put his leather glove on the handle. "This is what happens now. The box on the left is everything ... including a confession from me of every single murder I've committed. If you turn the crank left, this box will open."

His gloved hand moved from the crank to the other box, running his fingers along the top. "The box on the right, however, is the new name and whereabouts of the man responsible for the death of your mother and the destruction of your family."

The cloaked man turned on the old furnace. It came to life with a rush of igniting gas. He turned and pointed to the box under Miguel's feet. "When I close that door a timer will count down from thirty minutes. That should give you plenty of time to decide which box to choose. After thirty minutes the bomb will arm with a beep and you then have one minute to choose. Then ... Boom!"

"One more thing, once you have chosen a box, the contents of the other will drop into this incinerator and be gone forever. Do you understand?"

Miguel nodded, "So what happens now?"

The cloaked man adjusted his hat and opened the door to leave. "You're a good man, Miguel. Your sister would have been proud of you. I, on the other hand, am not so sure."

"For me, this is the path I've chosen and I don't intend to stray from it. It's all I have left. I will give you one piece of advice though. Whatever choice you make today, consider the consequences of how you decide to deal with it. You may start to enjoy it, and that's not a path you want to go down."

"Goodbye, Miguel. Maybe I'll see you around." He politely tipped his hat and walked out of the door, closing it with a creak.

Chapter 12

The Wages of Sin

November 5th, 2007

The two men sat on the curb watching vehicles pull in and out of the small truck-stop in Tye, Texas. Bored with their lives in an Arkansas trailer park, the duo had decided to take their show on the road in the form of a nationwide crime spree that included theft, murder, and carjacking as they moved from state to state.

The older of the two, Ray Crocker, spotted a man who appeared to have problems walking as he climbed out of his Kenworth cabover and began fueling the big truck.

"Hey, Matt, check out the guy in the green truck … he looks like he's hurt pretty bad. You ready?" He turned to look at his accomplice who was staring at a large white owl on the corner of the truckstop awning.

Angered by his partner's wandering mind, he reached over and slapped the small-framed man on the back of his head. "Hey, Bitch! Are you listening to me?"

Matthew cowered at the blow and turned to his partner, "Yeah, I'm listening! It's just that owl up there. It looks like the one I had a dream about a few nights ago."

Ray looked hard at the majestic bird. Its large round eyes shown like giant emeralds as they reflected the truckstop parking lot lights. A chill ran through him as he thought about Matt's comment about seeing the owl in his dreams. He, too, had dreamt of a similar animal a few months prior, but he wouldn't exactly call it a dream … a nightmare would be a better description. His eyes moved back to Matt who again was entranced by the bird.

Enraged, Ray picked up a glass bottle out of a trashcan and hurled it at the owl. The bottle smacked the great white bird in the side, knocking it off balance. The owl turned towards Ray. Its massive wings flapped as the bird directed its stare into Ray's eyes, causing him to take a step backwards.

As the white owl launched from the building and disappeared into the night, Matthew turned to Ray with a puzzled look on his face. "What did you do that for?"

Ray answered by grabbing him by the shirt collar and shaking him. "This ain't the Discovery Channel! We have to get a ride out of here before the cops find us! So get your shit together or I'll leave your sorry ass here! Got it!"

Matt quickly nodded in wide-eyed acknowledgement.

Ray let go of his shirt collar and began laying out the details of the plan. "We'll do this just like we did in Little Rock. I'll shoot him when we get down the road. You reach over him and grab the wheel. Piece of cake! Think you can handle that, Retard?"

Matt fearfully agreed and then looked at the intended victim who was busy washing the semi's windows. Matt had never really wanted to take part in the crimes he and his partner had committed, but he was afraid of Ray. He had watched him kill four people just over the last month and knew firsthand what Ray was capable of. Several times he had wanted to run but the thought of what Ray would do to him if caught was worse than the prison rapes he would endure if they were arrested together. So he was stuck … stuck with Ray to the uncertain end.

The two men began their con routine, complete with fake tears, and headed towards the cloaked man at the fuel pump.

The fedora-hatted man turned from the fuel pump as the two distraught-appearing men approached him. The older of the two walked up to him and pulled out his wallet. "Sir! Me and my son here need to get to Van Horn. My wife has been in a bad wreck and our car broke down. Please, can you help us get there? I have money; I can pay you. Can you help us?"

The cloaked man analyzed the two. Although they appeared sincere, he sensed something was not right. He paused for a moment, contemplating the stranger's words, and replied in a soft voice, "Ok, I'll take you. Wait here while I go pay for my fuel."

Ray continued his theatrical performance as he buried his head in the man's coated arm. "God bless you, Sir! You don't know how much this means to us."

The cloaked man shook his head and pulled away from Ray who continued to conjure up fake tears while gushing out his appreciation.

"No problem, I don't mind giving you two a ride. Just let me pay for my fuel and we'll go." The cloaked man patted Ray on the shoulder and limped towards the truckstop.

Ray waited until the man was out of earshot and quietly whispered to his partner. "This guy's a sucker. We'll be doing him a favor by killing him. Besides, did you see that roll of cash he has on him? We'll be living like kings in Mexico on that loot."

Matt looked at the cloaked man as he opened the truckstop door, then back to Ray. "I don't know, man, that guy is big! I have a bad feeling about this man."

Ray shook his head at Matt's words and patted his jacket pocket where his .32 caliber revolver was secreted. "Don't worry about that, bro … I got that covered."

The door chimed as the cloaked man walked in and approached the counter. A young woman stood staring out of the window at the two men.

"Are you going to give those two a ride?" she questioned, smacking her gum.

The cloaked man nodded, "I suppose so … they seem harmless enough."

The young woman shook her head and rang up the sale. "I'd watch myself, Honey. They've been out here all day trying to get a ride to El Paso. Something about their granddad was in the hospital. Is that the story they gave you?"

The cloaked man turned his head towards the two smiling men, narrowing his eyes at the two strangers standing by his truck. "Yep, that's what they told me. I'll get them where they need to go. Thanks for the heads up though, there're a lot of bad people out there." He tipped his hat and headed back to his truck.

He controlled his growing temper as he limped back towards the semi and approached the two men, his gray trench coat flapping gently in the cold wind that blew across the concrete parking lot.

"You fellows ready?" he asked in a faked pleasant voice as he opened the truck door.

"Yes, Sir! We're ready. Thanks again, man, we really appreciate it," came the reply.

The cloaked man nodded as he opened the truck passenger door and watched the two get inside. He shut the door and walked around the truck clenching his teeth in anger.

"Stupid bastards. Wrong place, wrong truck," he murmured to himself as he walked to the driver side and climbed up into the cab.

"Man, you don't know how much we appreciate this!" Ray thanked the trucker again.

A few miles had clicked by when the cloaked man slid his Ka-Bar Warthog knife out, holding it to his side and out of sight. He turned and looked at the boy in the bunk whose face was wet with sweat. "Hey, back there, what's your name?"

"Matthew … my name is Matthew," the young man answered in a jittery voice.

The cloaked man clutched the knife tightly in his hand, readying himself. He looked over to his right at the passenger side window. A flash of chrome reflected off the glass as Ray pulled the hidden .32 pistol out of his pocket.

"So, what hospital is your grandpa in?" the killer asked, feigning chitchat.

Ray reverted to his heartrending act and answered, "I don't know yet. All we know is that he's in Van Ho …"

Ray's voice ceased as he realized what the cloaked man had asked and that he had been caught. He looked out of the corner of his eye at the trucker straightening himself up in the driver's seat.

A sneer came across Ray's face as he whipped out the revolver and shoved the barrel against the cloaked man's head. "Alright, Motherfucker! This is what's goin' down!" he screamed, pulling back the hammer on the pistol.

The killer laughed aloud, "What're you going to do? Kill me?"

Ray fired back, "You damn right, Motherfucker! Now pull the truck over!"

The trucker continued to laugh as he held the accelerator to the floor.

As the huge semi gained speed, Ray looked over at the speedometer that was now reading well over a hundred miles per hour. "I'm serious, Bitch! Pull the truck over!"

"Are you scared yet?" the cloaked man bellowed as the eighteen-wheeler screamed down the long stretch of road.

Ray sneered at the man and cocked the hammer back. "This is it, Motherfucker! One more chance! Pull it over!" he screamed.

The cloaked man turned his eyes to the frightened man holding the pistol. He looked hard into the barrel of the gun and smiled. Then he hit the brakes with a hard stomp, sending Ray's head flying into the windshield with a bloody smack and the boy in the bunk hurling into the dash, knocking him out cold. The killer instantly raised his knife and slashed at Ray, cutting his arm to the bone.

Ray's eyes widened in shock as he dropped the pistol and grabbed his bleeding arm. He looked over at the man who was again drawing back the knife, this time to thrust it into his throat.

Realizing he was beaten, he shoved the semi's passenger door open and threw himself out of the speeding truck and to the ground with a thud.

He stumbled to his feet and began running down the highway. Fear shot through him as he heard the diesel engine gun, the big rig whipping around in his direction. Ray began to run faster at the thought that the man was going to run him down.

The cloaked man's teeth were clinched in anger as he found the running con-man in his headlights. He clicked the transmission into high range and stomped on the accelerator.

As the truck got closer, the running man turned and headed out into the desert in hopes the driver would abandon the chase. He had thought wrong as the cabover bounced off the paved road and into the desert sand, kicking up a cloud of dust under the churning wheels as the driver shifted gears.

Ray's heart raced as he blindly ran full-speed into the dark night.

Then, just ahead of him, illuminated by the truck's headlights, he spotted a group of boulders. If he could make it to them, he might have a chance.

Ray turned his head towards the truck, not noticing a creosote bush directly in his path. He barreled headlong into the plant, tangling up his feet and falling to the ground.

The speeding truck was now on him. Its loud, revving motor drowned out his painful wail as the tires rolled over his legs, breaking them like toothpicks.

The air in the brake pods released as the truck came to a grinding halt in the sand. The killer climbed down from the cab and began whistling as he strolled over to the whimpering criminal. "Looks like you have a big problem," he said as he knelt down over the broken man.

Ray looked up at him and sneered, "Fuck you, man! Go ahead ... kill me! You think I'm scared?"

The cloaked man pulled out Ray's own dropped revolver and pointed at his face.

The injured man on the ground cringed and whimpered as he heard the hammer click back.

"Yeah, I think you're scared. To be honest, you're not worth the bullet. I'll let the coyotes take care of you," answered the With that, he shoved the pistol back in his pocket and limped back to his truck, put it in gear with a crunch and turned the semi back towards the highway.

"Yeah, that's what I thought, Bitch! Run off!" Ray shouted as the truck's taillights disappeared into the dust-filled night air.

He lay there for a few minutes, trying to figure out what to do. He knew he had to get help soon. The pain in his mangled legs was growing more intense by the second, and his slashed arm was bleeding profusely.

He began to crawl, but stopped when he heard something moving close by in the darkness. He listened to the dark desert and heard heavy, dog-like panting all around him. He thought about the cloaked man's words about leaving him to the coyotes.

Then he remembered growing up in the hills of Arkansas where he had always heard that coyotes wouldn't attack a human and if you made enough noise, they would run away. Hoping it was true, he began to yell and throw rocks in the direction of the sound, hoping to scare away whatever it was.

Just then, for a moment, the clouds moved away from the moon, illuminating the arid desert. To his horror, the form of a cougar stood no more than fifteen feet from him.

He frantically crawled backwards, hollering at the animal, but the cat was unwavering in his slow pacing as it moved steadily towards the injured man.

Ray's face was a picture of terror as he looked into the cougar's glowing green eyes. It hunched to pounce and leaped into the air.

There was no one to hear Ray's screams as the hungry animal turned the criminal into the night's banquet.

The truck bounced back onto the highway, the driver whistling as he drove into the night. It had been years since he had been in the old semi. He recalled the money and time he had spent in it. Seldom visited memories of his former career came back as he looked around the interior of the cab.

His eyes came to rest on the CD player. It's orange light indicated that there was a CD loaded in the machine. "Hmm," he commented as he reached out with his gloved hand and pressed the play button. An old favorite tune came through the speakers, "Rock and Roll All Night" by KISS, making him smile.

His mind wandered back to the time before his life was taken from him. A welcome moment of levity came over him, and he felt like a human again. He turned the volume up and headed towards Sierra Blanca.

Chapter 13

Pawn Takes King

November 7th, 2007

Carlos Mentaga sat upstairs in his lounge chair staring out the window at the orange glow of the sun as it rose. He looked as if he was enjoying the morning, unscathed by any outside distractions as he sipped his coffee. Mentaga closed his eyes, letting the sun shine on his face, but his peaceful appearance was a false one.

For the past few weeks his sleep has been plagued with nightmares, horrible visions of a cloaked man that appeared out of a wall of fire. In the reoccurring dream the intruder wanted not only to take his life, but take his soul as well.

He first thought of it as only a bad dream until he saw that damned video. The disturbing dream became reality as he watched the recording, a reality that made him feel something he had rarely felt in his life … fear.

Carlos' troubled thoughts were replaced by a strange feeling that he was being watched. He opened his eyes slowly and blinked at an image in the open window. Perched on the windowsill was a large white owl. Its large predatory eyes stared into Carlos' panic-stricken face as he rocked backwards in his chair, tilting it over backwards.

"Enyo! *Enyo!* Help me!" he screamed as he scrambled across the floor in an attempt to get away from the omen of death.

The summoned bodyguard came running into the room with his pistol drawn and found his employer huddled into a quivering ball on the floor. "What's wrong, Senor Carlos?" he questioned.

Just then, the large bird in the opening let out a haunting hoot making Enyo's blood run cold. He took a step back as the owl extended its wings and launched itself from the window into the morning air.

Enyo thought of the story told by the delirious survivor of the slaughter at Darrel King's mansion. The man had told Enyo he had a dream that the "Buho Blanco", an old Indian legend of a messenger of death in the form of a white owl, warned him that they would all pay for the things they had done. At the time, he thought the man, being close to death, was imagining things, but now he began to think differently.

Carlos looked up at Enyo and stammered, "Is ... is it gone?"

He nodded, "Yes, Senor Carlos, it is gone."

Enyo had the feeling that his employer was losing his grip. Nightly, Mentaga would wake up screaming about some man taking his soul. The nightmares and the fact that every day a package would arrive with a body part of a "13" gangster inside were breaking the morale of the guards that Carlos had hired to fortify his mansion.

Carlos began to pace wildly around the room, muttering to himself.

With Carlos in this agitated state, Enyo dreaded what he had to tell him next.

"Senor Carlos, I have some bad news. The Wolf is dead. They found him three days ago ... shot to hell."

Carlos went ballistic at the news, picking up a lamp from his table and hurling it out of the same window where the white owl had sat. "Who is this bastard? What the hell did I do to deserve this? I tell you what, Enyo, I will find him myself and when I do, I will skin him alive!"

Carlos flashed his crazed eyes at Enyo and barked his orders. "Get the men ready, Enyo. If this, this ghost, shows up, I want his head on a fucking platter! Understand?"

"Yes, Senor Carlos, I will get right on it," the henchman answered meekly.

Later in the day as he entered the main room, he looked at the alerted guards who were joking and laughing. If this man was able to kill the Wolf, what chance did these men stand against the killer he wondered? These men were only useful for dealing with rival gangs and unarmed citizens.

Enyo pulled out his weapon, a .357 Ruger pistol, and checked the cylinder. Although he was not superstitious, he was not going to take any chances. The White Owl in the window had scared him. He holstered the pistol and walked outside past the gates, listening to the quiet desert. His eyes moved to the West where he watched the evening sun disappear over the horizon. He felt strange as if eyes were bearing down on him from somewhere in the desert.

He focused on a hill in the distance for a few seconds. He thought he had seen something move but was not sure. A shudder ran through his body as he snapped out of his trance.

"You are seeing things, Enyo," he said to himself as he turned and walked back into the compound.

On a sandy hill some half a mile away, the hard eyes of the killer sized up the compound through his binoculars.

"Fifteen outside, probably more inside. If this were Hollywood, it would be easy," he muttered as he slipped back behind the top of the hill and down to the tractor-trailer rig parked below.

It was almost time to end Carlos' life, a task that he had been looking forward to for the last seven years. His gloved hands opened the trailer door with a creak. He pulled out a set of ramps and quietly off-loaded a cargo van that had been loaded inside.

As he idled the vehicle, the killer's hands moved to the Franchi SPAS-15 assault shotgun that lay across the passenger seat. He shouldered it as he slowly pulled the van out in the direction of Carlos' compound.

His eyes narrowed as he calculated the distance to the encampment and began the task of readying the vehicle for its trip through the large gates that protected the mansion.

"This should be it," he thought to himself as he reached between the seats and flipped a toggle switch. The glow of tiny green LEDs illuminated the van's interior as the gelled fuel bomb's arming mechanism came to life. The killer counted them and smiled, "I have a surprise for you, Carlos, and you're going to love it."

The black-leaded glove reached to the dash and grabbed a remote device that controlled an electronic steering assembly in the van. He moved the joystick and watched closely at the wheels turn.

"Perfect!" he thought to himself as he exited the van, locked the accelerator to the floor and pulled the breakaway shifting lever into drive, sending the rolling bomb racing towards the compound.

Enyo had just stepped inside the mansion when a voice from one of the outside guards rang out. He turned to see a white van in a cloud of dust hurtling towards the house.

"Oh God! He is here! The Ghost has come!" Enyo exclaimed to himself, racing towards the staircase to alert Carlos.

Carlos' outside guards quickly huddled together at the front gate to defend the compound. Unaware of the deadly contents inside the fast-approaching vehicle, they began to relentlessly pour hot lead from the barrels of their submachine guns into the front of the van as it crashed through the gates and slammed into the house.

The guards shouted and continued to fire at the disabled vehicle as a black big rig sped unnoticed through the dust cloud created by the van and stopped about a hundred yards from the front gate.

The killer readied the remote and watched as the guards stopped firing, moving towards the van with their weapons drawn.

"Checkmate," the killer said quietly as he hit the button, igniting the combination of high explosives, gelled gasoline, and ball bearings. The bomb exploded in a violent surge of flame and shrapnel, consuming the approaching guards. The powerful blast ripped them into streams of blood and burning flesh, spewing body parts in all directions.

With a whip of his trench coat, the killer was out of the rig and moving towards the house. His eyes were fixed on the burning doorway as he raised the SPAS-15 to his shoulder.

By now, the inside guards were making their way out of the house. He pulled the trigger of the semi-automatic shotgun and released a swarm of armor-piercing slugs from the twenty-round magazine into the bewildered men, springing geysers of blood as the deadly rounds pounded them like sledgehammers.

The black, flat-nosed boots clicked hard on the concrete walkway as the cloaked man hurriedly crossed the wide yard and dove behind a brick column to escape a volley of gunfire that blasted from the left side of the courtyard.

"Damn it!" he winched as he felt a burning sensation on his back from the bullets that hammered his Kevlar-lined trench coat. He glanced around the brick column to see three men using their chattering machine guns to keep him pinned down.

As they moved closer, the killer reached into a large pocket of his trench coat and pulled out a cylindrical explosive. He hit the recessed arming toggle and tossed the cylinder in the general vicinity of the guards. The bomb went off with a thunderous blast, giving the killer time to act as the three momentarily stunned men hunkered down from the explosion. The killer jumped from behind the brick column and quickly triggered his massive shotgun, sending a hail of fletchettes pouring into the guards. As the spinning steel darts ripped their bodies, they contorted in pain and dropped lifeless to the ground.

He ran to the side of the open mansion door as bullets spattered around him from inside. "How many can be left?" he thought to himself, slipping off a satchel that he carried on his back. He waited until he heard the sound of footsteps close to the burning door. Arming the device, he flung the beeping satchel into the faces of the remaining five guards.

The defenders tried to run from the flying bag, letting out helpless yelps as the device holding ten pounds of nails and five pounds of explosives exploded in mid air, severing limbs and tearing chunks out of their dying bodies. The screaming five-inch nails tumbling through the air had found their marks.

The killer waited for a moment as the wails of the men inside the house became silent. Then he slowly crept through the burning door with the SPAS-15 held tightly against his shoulder. As he moved quietly through the battered front room of the mansion, a violent impact spun him around, causing him to drop the shotgun to the floor. He peered at the weapon, seeing a hole through the action where one of Enyo's pistol rounds had struck, rendering it useless. He reached for his .45 only to be hit with another devastating round to his chest. The killer grabbed at the wound and looked up toward the sound of a laughing Enyo

Emerging from his hiding place, Enyo taunted, "Some ghost, huh? You almost had me believing it for a second but, from the looks of things, I would say you are just a man. What a shame. We could have used a man like you." Enyo snapped up his pistol and fired again, striking the man-killer once more in the chest and knocking him to the ground.

Enyo smiled and walked over to an intercom on the wall. He pressed the call button and summoned Carlos, who was tucked away in a safe room at the back of the house.

"Senor Mentaga, are you there?" the speaker crackled as Carlos' voice came through.

"Is he dead? Did you get him?" came the response.

Enyo nodded and replied, "Yes, Senor Carlos, he is de ..."

Enyo's words were cut short as his blinking eyes rested on a blood spatter on the white wall in front of him. He looked down to see a growing area of red on his sport jacket. He turned slowly to see the cloaked man standing in front of him. His trench coat was open, exposing the steel reinforced vest underneath. His eyes moved to two small red patches that ringed two protruding bullets stuck in its fibrous weave.

"Always check your shots, Enyo," the cloaked man said as he squeezed the trigger, sending the round into Enyo's head. A wide splatter of blood and brain fanned on the wall behind Enyo. His lifeless body swayed for a moment, then fell into the bloody puddle on the floor beneath him.

The killer looked at the dead man for a moment, then his piercing eyes shot to the intercom on hearing Carlos' frustrated voice come over the speaker.

"Enyo! Enyo! Did you kill him or not! Answer me, Cavron!" He released the button for Enyo to answer but another voice came through the speaker into the safe room … a voice that chilled him to the bone.

"Hello, Carlos. Are you comfortable in there?"

Carlos' face twitched in anger as he slammed his fist into the intercom talk button. "Who are you? What do you want?" He let go of the button only to hear a chuckle from the other end.

"I'll give you the answer to that in 10 … 9 … 8 …"

As he counted down, Carlos stepped away from the intercom with a puzzled look on his face. He thought for a moment, then turned his eyes to the steel door. "Fuck!" he screamed as he realized why the man was counting down.

Carlos turned and dove away from the door, but it was too late. The massive explosive planted on the other side of the door burst it open, sending a large, swirling piece of wrenched metal into Carlos's leg, slicing it off at the knee. The blast wave hurled him sideways into the concrete wall of the safe room, smashing his ribs and arm from the impact.

The acrid smell of smoke filled Carlos' nostrils. As he choked and opened his eyes, he witnessed the details of his reoccurring horrible nightmare unfold in front of him as the cloaked man stepped through the flaming doorway, crossing the gap between them with his echoing footsteps.

Carlos sneered and pulled up his Desert Eagle pistol to shoot but his arm, broken at the elbow, cracked and folded at the break. Carlos howled in pain as the cloaked man knelt down and spoke in a sarcastic tone, "Damn! I'll bet that hurt!"

Carlos lifted his head and spat a bubble of blood onto the killer's trench coat in reply. "Fuck you, Cavron! Do you think I am scared of you?"

The killer chuckled, grabbed Carlos by his remaining leg and, with a powerful jerk, pulled him out of the smoke-filled room into the main hall where Carlos' guards lay strewn about the blood-covered floor.

"Lovely party we're having here, Carlos! It would've been a shame if you'd missed it."

The killer dropped Carlos' leg and pulled out a long dagger from inside the trench coat.

"What are you going to do?" Carlos screamed as the killer grabbed his broken arm and slid him up the wall.

"We're going to play a game, Carlos. I like to call it "Senseless Violence". You know how to play, don't you?"

Carlos's pain-stricken face melted with fear as the killer raised the dagger and plunged it through Carlos's hand and into the wooden wall behind. Carlos cried out, twisting in agony. The combination of his wounds and the freshly pierced hand hit him all at once as he painfully hung from the dagger.

The killer reached into his trench coat and brought out a photo of himself and his family, shoving it into Carlos' face as he shouted, "Do you recognize these two, Carlos? The woman was my wife! Her name was Mayella and you shot her. The little girl's name was Isabella. You disemboweled her and packed her full of your poison! That is who I am! And you, I want you, and everyone who knows you, to die! That is what I want!"

The killer took the photo and stuffed it into Carlos' mouth. "Here! Take this with you to Hell!"

Carlos let out a muffled cry as the cloaked man pulled the singing metallic blade of his Ka-Bar knife from its sheath and thrust it downward, slicing Carlos from his chest to his hip and sending a spray of blood fanning from the razor-sharp blade as Carlos' entrails spilled onto the blood-splattered floor.

The cloaked man's rage was as yet unquenched as he began to violently slash Carlos' face over and over, madly laughing as the blood flew from the still barely alive gang leader's body. He continued to cut until he had no strength left.

Exhausted, the killer stepped back, and looked at what was left of Carlos' dead body. Breathing heavily, he fell back against the wall and stared at the lifeless corpse for what seemed like an eternity.

For a moment he felt a sense of finality. A sense of peace like the weight of the world had been lifted from his shoulders, but in the serene silence he knew that this was far from over. Carlos was a big fish, but there is always a bigger fish. His employers would be vengeful. They would want some reparation for all they had lost. No, it was not over … it was only the beginning.

He raised himself from the wall and slowly limped outside into the desert air. As he slowly made his way to the semi-truck he turned towards the mansion. He thought for a moment about torching it like he had done to every other house or building he had assaulted. Not this time. He would leave this scene of death as a warning for the rest of the "13" and their affiliates. A warning of what was to come.

Chapter 14

The Game Begins

November 4th, 2007–4 pm

Replaying the conversation with the cloaked figure over and over in his mind, Miguel's eyes were fixed on the crank handle between the two metal boxes welded to the top of the aged crematory furnace. The timer clock on the explosives ticked away the seconds to either his death or his freedom.

Miguel had a choice to make … and soon.

Leaving Miguel with his options, the cloaked man cracked a smile as he looked at the whimsical device atop the old incinerator and left the room. He knew which box Miguel was going to choose. He could have just laid its contents on the table but he had given him a choice … to have the killer's confession and evidence that would send him to death row, bringing an end to the six years of chasing this ghost of a man, or information that would lead Miguel to the man responsible for his family's demise.

As time ran out, the clock zeroed and a loud beep sounded as the bomb armed, leaving him only a single minute to act. Miguel painfully stood up and staggered over to the machine. He reached in between the two steel containers and turned the handle.

The door sprang open for the box he had chosen while the contents of the other dropped into the fiery furnace just as the killer had said. He snatched the bag from the open container and quickly headed for the door.

As he reached for the doorknob to make his escape, something caught his eye. He stepped over to the chessboard, reached down and lifted a single chess piece that stood alone on one side of the board. He looked back at the timer ticking away with only seconds remaining.

Ignoring the numbness in his legs and the pain in his side, he quickly made his way out the door and ran down the hallway, hoping to escape the impending blast.

As he reached the end of the tunnel-like structure, he dove to one side as a massive cloud of flame and steel shards belched from the doorway like an erupting volcano.

Once outside, Miguel breathed a sigh of relief as he lay in the cold grass and let the tingling in his legs subside. With a heave, he pulled himself upright and looked around at his surroundings.

To his amazement, there was a running car with the driver's door opened.

Miguel cocked his head and walked over to the idling vehicle. Any other time this would seem unbelievably strange but after this day's events, nothing surprised him. The warmed vehicle was a soothing sight. He slid behind the wheel and leaned back in the seat.

"Wake up, Miguel!" he coaxed. As his exhausted eyes looked over to the passenger seat, he saw a large crate with a note on top. He picked up the piece of paper and began to read, "I need you to do me a favor, Miguel. This crate contains evidence and the names of dozens of people involved with the "13" gang in the United States. Make sure it gets in the right hands."

Miguel put the letter down and looked at the sealed bag in his other hand that he had pulled from the incinerator's right side steel box. Did he really even want to look? Years had passed since the monster he had called his father came home drunk and beat his mother to death. If what the cloaked man had said was true, he now held the whereabouts of the man that had destroyed his family with the swing of a fist, and taken him far away from his home, only to leave him for dead on the side of the road.

Miguel slowly opened the bag and pulled out the stapled contents. He began flipping through the pages when three pictures fell into his lap. He looked down at them in horror as the repressed memory of his family's downfall flashed vividly in his mind.

His eyes fixed on the image of a man in one of the photos. He picked up the picture and stared hard at it. A rush of anger came over him as he looked into the face of his father. The stern face was the same as he remembered in his nightmares, only the fear he once felt when he looked into his father's cold blue eyes was now gone.

Miguel knew what he had to do now, but first, he had to get this box of evidence back to the Bureau. The crate was full of information that would blow the top off of more than half of the cocaine rings in the nation.

Then he would take care of the man that ruined his life.

Miguel walked out of the meeting room tired, but liberated. He had delivered the box of damning evidence to his superiors, who were more than happy to begin using the proof it contained to start a massive manhunt for the gang members listed in the documents.

As he walked down the long, quiet corridor to his office, the voice of Director Galvan rang out behind him, "Miguel, wait!"

Miguel turned with a surprised look as Rafael ran down the hallway. "What's wrong?" he asked as Rafael grabbed him by the shoulder.

"No time! I need you to come with me! They got your guy! The motel killer! The local police shot him a few minutes ago in Van Horn! They're sending over some live images of the crime scene for you to ID the body."

Miguel's stomach drew in a knot as he reluctantly followed Rafael into the briefing room where an agent was pulling up the live feed cam on the computer. He turned to Rafael and asked, "How did they find him?"

Rafael turned with a smile. "Some bum called the local police. Said he rented a room at his seedy motel to a guy that was carrying a pistol and a laptop computer. The Van Horn boys in blue showed up to check it out and caught the guy, sleeping on the bed with three corpses stacked in the corner. They say he went for his gun so they shot him. Sad thing ... after all that evidence he turned you on to."

He turned and saw Miguel's dismayed face as the young agent waited for the images to appear on the computer. He patted him on the shoulder, saying, "Don't feel bad, Miguel, the man was a psychopath. You should feel lucky you made it out alive. Evidence or no evidence, he was still a murderer."

Miguel nodded as the agent at the computer announced that the video was loading. He raised his head and looked at the dead man that lay on the blood-spattered bed. He smiled as he saw the scraggly, bug-eyed form with a .45 in his hand.

"What was his name?" Miguel asked.

"They've identified him as a Matthew Morris from Y City, Arkansas. He has a record a mile long."

"That's him. That's the guy." Miguel said as the smile on his face turned into a chuckle. "I should have known it wasn't you," he thought to himself as the agent sent the response.

Hearing Miguel's chuckle, Rafael looked curiously at him. "What's so funny?"

Miguel waved his hand, shaking his head, "Nothing, Sir. I'm just happy it's over. After all of this, I think I need a vacation. I've got some business to attend to."

Rafael cocked his head and shrugged, "Start it today, if you like. You deserve it."

Miguel walked out of the office and down the long hallway towards the front door of the Bureau. Miguel's mind was a cloud of anger, relief and confusion. He would now be able to help his long-dead sister and mother's souls rest in peace. The information the mystery man had given him was enough to find the man responsible for his pain-filled life and he would attend to him … soon.

The remaining question burning in his brain was about the cloaked man's true identity. Who was he?

As he opened the glass door that led to the parking lot, Miguel stopped, reached into his trousers and pulled out the chess piece he had taken from the old crematory basement. He studied it for a moment. It was expensive … real gold … real silver. Someone had to custom-make the piece. Maybe that was where to start.

He looked over the figurine perched on top of the cracked pawn once more. It was a large owl with its wings spread as it grasped the pawn with its talons. He had always been a big fan of history and recalled reading old English folklore that spoke of a White Owl, known as a Harpier, that would come as a messenger of death. He held the chess piece close to his eyes.

"Harpier's Pawn!" he muttered as he stepped into his car and headed home.

To be continued …

Credits

Bill Ward of Ward's Concept Art for the spectacular book cover ... you are a genius dude!
The OTR truckers with whom I have shared the highways for many years.
The crew of Missouri Petroleum who insisted that I write a book.
My Grandfather for all of his wonderful stories when I was a child.
My friends and family who also insisted that I write a book.
My uncle, Lewis Suttles, for taking the time to help me with writing this book. Without him it would have not been possible.
Finally, to the purchaser. You are buying more than just a book. You are buying a testament of people who have lost and continue to lose their lives every day to the drug trade and to the children of the world who are preyed upon by sick individuals who seek only to destroy their lives. They must not be forgotten.

Thank You
Daniel Christian Green

978-0-595-46067-0
0-595-46067-4

www.ingramcontent.com/pod-product-compliance
Ingram Content Group UK Ltd.
Pitfield, Milton Keynes, MK11 3LW, UK
UKHW041958230426
12048UKWH00008B/405